HAPPINESS FOREVER

HAPPINESS FOREVER

A NOVEL

ADELAIDE FAITH

FARRAR, STRAUS AND GIROUX   NEW YORK

Farrar, Straus and Giroux
120 Broadway, New York 10271

Printed in the United States of America
First edition, 2025

Grateful acknowledgment is made for permission to reprint lines from
Hope Of The States' "Left," 2006, courtesy of Sam Herlihy.

Title-page hand-lettering by Na Kim.

Library of Congress Cataloging-in-Publication Data
Names: Faith, Adelaide, 1975– author.
Title: Happiness forever : a novel / Adelaide Faith.
Description: First edition. | New York : Farrar, Straus and Giroux, 2025.
Identifiers: LCCN 2024049360 | ISBN 9780374608668 (hardcover)
Subjects: LCGFT: Novels.
Classification: LCC PR6106.A46 H37 2025 | DDC 823/.92—
    dc23/eng/20241210
LC record available at https://lccn.loc.gov/2024049360

Designed by Abby Kagan

Our books may be purchased in bulk for promotional, educational, or business
use. Please contact your local bookseller or the Macmillan Corporate and
Premium Sales Department at 1-800-221-7945, extension 5442, or by email at
MacmillanSpecialMarkets@macmillan.com.

www.fsgbooks.com
Follow us on social media at @fsgbooks

1   3   5   7   9   10   8   6   4   2

For Fawn

A person can waste their whole life, without even meaning to, all because another person has a really great face.

—SHEILA HETI, *Pure Colour*

What you want you're never gonna get
Unless you are prepared to be alone
If you think you've got to have it all
You've got to be prepared to give it up

—"Left," Hope Of The States

HAPPINESS FOREVER

1

COBWEBS

THE ROOM feels like the base of a cheesecake. Sylvie sits
down, rolls up her shirtsleeves, looks at the box of tissues.
The therapist is standing in the doorway of the therapy room
holding two glasses of water. She is tall and slim, has slender
exposed wrists, wears a thick gold ring on her middle finger,
like a king. She is smiling, but she has to smile.

Coming up to the therapy room, Sylvie's shoes had made
the sound of *one, two, three, shake your body down, shake it all
down,* on the wooden stairs, and the song still loops, silently,
inside her head. She looks at the therapist—her face, her hair,
her hands—and tries, not for the first time, to work out how
old she is. Sylvie wants a rough age, so she can have an end
date in mind for her obsession. If the therapist is approaching sixty now, the obsession shouldn't last more than twenty

years, max. Sylvie doubts she would feel desperate to touch an eighty-year-old's body, however beautiful they were.

"You look deep in thought. What's on your mind?" the therapist says, still smiling, as she puts down the glasses of water on their separate tables.

The room is plain and calm, but Sylvie feels a mild unease knowing she can't leave. She feels stuck in her chair, the chair legs stuck to the floor. Still, she doesn't want to leave, would prefer never to have to leave at all, and it's a feeling that's sickly and sweet. Today is her thirteenth session. She feels she's revealed a lot about herself already, but she barely knows anything about the therapist; she doesn't know what the therapist likes to do, for example. She knows a little bit about what the therapist's husband likes to do, because he has a blog. He likes drinking whiskey and watching documentaries and painting landscapes. But all Sylvie knows about the therapist, apart from what qualifications she has and where she got them, is what she can see on the surface of her body— the bandage on her hand that turned out to be covering a dog bite, the change in the color of her long straight hair from gray to peach.

"I was thinking about Nick," Sylvie says.

Sylvie told the therapist last session that the therapy room reminds her of Nick's bedroom. Nick had been Sylvie's boyfriend when she was seventeen and still at school. In Nick's room, Sylvie had rolled around on the floor, smoked Camel Lights, sucked the horn-of-plenty pendant that was on his necklace. In the therapy room, she sits still in her chair and just talks, yet somehow it feels the same. The therapist had suggested that both rooms felt like contained worlds, separate from the rest of her life, with separate rules. Sylvie had said she had the feeling that she was being saved from everybody else in these two rooms. From her parents in Nick's room, and from her contemporaries in the therapy room.

The therapist wears a different outfit every week and Sylvie wonders if she does this on purpose, so Sylvie won't be able to appropriate her style and try to look like her, for comfort, if she wants to. Today the therapist is wearing a cream blouse with a bow, gray trousers, and a gray cardigan.

"I was thinking about this time," Sylvie is saying, "when we were lying on Nick's floor with a blanket over us. We were messing around, but Nick stopped and pushed the blanket upward with both hands and said he was trying to get out of the cobwebs. I remember thinking he was talking on a deeper level than other people, and I felt so happy with him then, and so happy with myself for my choice of boyfriend. I remember thinking, *My mum would never understand Nick, but I understand him, he's referencing the 'Lullaby' video*—the video for this single that had just come out," Sylvie says.

The therapist nods.

"But it was me that didn't understand," Sylvie goes on. "Nick probably thought he *was* stuck in cobwebs because he was high. He wasn't trying to impress me with his knowledge of a music video, and he wasn't being metaphorical."

"Did you know he was taking drugs?" the therapist asks.

"No," Sylvie says. "He never took anything in front of me, I had no idea. Then one time, when I was sitting on his knee on the merry-go-round at the park, he said, 'Do you know every time you've seen me, I've been out of my mind on a different drug?' I couldn't believe it. I didn't understand why he'd been keeping it secret, or why he waited until then to tell me."

"Did he ask you to take drugs with him after that?"

"Yes!" Sylvie gets a mint out of her bag. She remembers Nick's front room when his parents were away. Charlotte there, closing the curtains, Nick and Hatstand on the sofa, their spoons ready on the low table, the feeling that she couldn't stay.

"He tried to get me to take heroin with him. He said we'd go into a different world. But I was too scared."

"I'm glad you were too scared," the therapist says. "It's something we have in common," she continues brightly.

"What, that we were both too scared to try heroin?" Sylvie asks, laughing.

"Yes!" the therapist answers, beaming.

2

AQUASCUTUM

SYLVIE HADN'T CHOSEN THE THERAPIST because she had found her attractive. She had chosen her because she was the only one, out of the twenty-three pages of local therapists Sylvie had scrolled through, who didn't strike her as too annoying to talk to. She had chosen her by default! At first Sylvie had related to the therapist as she would relate to one of her mum's friends, maybe mixed with a doctor. But then she had seen her outside of the therapy room.

Sylvie and the therapist had both been walking their dogs on the crown of the hill. They were walking toward each other, and Sylvie was conscious that they were like mirror images, both attached to a small white dog on a black leash. The therapist was dressed in peach, some kind of checked fabric, buttoned up, and above her coat there was the shape of her long straight hair and sunglasses. Sylvie wasn't sure if she was seeing correctly in the moment, and wasn't sure if she was re-calling correctly afterward. She didn't feel that she could trust herself. But the feeling she got then, seeing the therapist, re-minded her of how she would hold her face up to the sun when she was little, and close her eyes. When the color of the light coming through her eyelids made her certain for the first time that the world was good.

Later, Sylvie wondered why she hadn't felt this in the ther-apy room, wondered how she'd been oblivious to the thera-pist's beauty there. Had she been too consumed by talking and crying? Had she been looking for too long at the curtains or into the corner of the room? Or maybe the therapist just looked really good in coat and sunglasses. Had she been wearing Aquascutum? In Sylvie's first session, the therapist had asked what Sylvie would prefer to do if they crossed paths in town. It was the client's choice, the therapist had said. Syl-vie had felt that she didn't care either way and opted for say-ing hello. But when it actually happened, when they were just about to cross paths, Sylvie's body had turned around and started running down the hill. She had picked up her dog, Curtains, who had brain damage and couldn't run on a leash, and held her to her chest as she ran.

Since that encounter, Sylvie's brain had brought up the image of *the therapist outside* multiple times a day. The coat, the hair, the sunglasses, the dog on a leash. The image made Sylvie feel as if she were about to uncover the key to some-thing big. She felt she might be saved if she followed the therapist, got her approval, made her love her. There was a sense that a great freedom was close. There might be no need to worry about carrying on when somebody else had already worked out the meaning of life, if the meaning of life was how to become the perfect human. The game, the puzzle, might be over. Whatever it was the key to, the image made Sylvie feel sharp and happy and insanely high.

The air outside Sylvie's house hummed from then on with the prospect of another sighting. She took her dog out for extra walks. But at night, when it was too dark to see another person's face, and when the therapist would be shut inside her house, Sylvie's body would start to ache. She could feel herself being pulled toward the bay window which led to the street that led to the therapist's house and she would find that she was moaning. She put her hands on the glass panes. She wanted to know what the therapist was doing. She wanted to know so she could measure it against what she was doing and, if possible, narrow the gap.

3

HEAD BAG

SYLVIE HAS MADE A PHOTOCOPY of a short story she just read. She is bringing it to therapy. The title of the story is "Therapy." Sylvie wants the therapist to read it so she can see how hard it is to be the client, to come to sessions knowing nothing about the therapist and leave the same way. The client in the story doesn't like the way their therapist walks down the corridor after each session—too quickly, too happily, instead of staying in the room to write notes. Sylvie folds the photocopy and puts it in her bag.

The therapist opens the door and Sylvie starts up the stairs and her shoes still make the sound of *one, two, three, shake your body down*, but it sounds faster today, a record put on at the wrong speed. Her body is fast and shaking and she doesn't know if this is because she is nervous about giving the therapist the story, or if it is because she has decided this will be the session when she tells the therapist that she can't stop thinking about her. The therapist puts two waters on separate tables and sits down. She is wearing brown tweed trousers and a cream turtleneck and her hair has a slight wave to it.

"What would you like to talk about today?" she says brightly, crossing her legs and smiling.

Looking at the therapist makes Sylvie feel as if she has just walked into an elegant hotel and is going to be brought something that is on fire, like a pudding. Sylvie turns her head and looks at the closed door. It is painted cream and looks heavy and seems as safe as a private doctor's door in the city, and Sylvie feels that she can go ahead.

"I keep wanting to talk to you about this thing," Sylvie says. She puts her hand in her bag to get a mint and the folded story pokes out and she pushes it back in quickly. Now that she is in the therapy room, it is obvious to Sylvie that she shouldn't use someone else's story to make her own point.

The therapist nods and waits. She is smiling at first, but then she leans back in her chair and does something with her mouth, as if something is baking in there, and her eyes get big and wet, and Sylvie realizes that the therapist is stifling a yawn. Sylvie pretends she hasn't noticed and hangs her head down. She won't tell her now. That insulting yawn, maybe it has power enough to break the spell. Maybe the therapist knew what Sylvie was about to say and stifled a yawn on purpose, at that exact point, to stop her from saying it. The therapist moves forward in her chair and smiles and slightly tilts her head. She has a navy page-a-day diary on her lap and she is twirling the ribbon from the diary around one finger and

Sylvie stares at this, seems to see it in slow motion. Her brain starts to replay it again and again, though she doesn't know where she gets this extra time from, what everyone else is doing when she gets this extra time, and Sylvie's desire for the therapist is reinstated again, like a bouncy castle quickly filled with air.

"Do you know that song 'Abracadabra'?" Sylvie says.

"I don't think so," the therapist says, smiling.

"I had to dance to it, for a performance. With the Girl Guides. When we moved house, my mum signed me up to Girl Guides to make friends, and they were already practicing the dance."

The therapist nods.

"We were dressed all in black, but we had white gloves that were glow-in-the-dark. And when the song went, *I wanna reach out and grab ya*, we had to throw our glowing hands out to the audience."

"And how did it go?" the therapist says.

"Fine, I think. I don't think I did anything wrong. I don't even know why I'm talking about this."

"Maybe there was something about that time that was hard for you. It can be difficult for a child to move house."

"I do picture an old man in the corner, watching the performance," Sylvie says. "But maybe everyone feels like that, to some extent, when they look back on their childhood."

"That an old man was watching them?" the therapist says. "Was there an old man?"

"Probably not *actually*. I just . . . I pictured an old man with white hair glowing in the dark, like one of our gloves, but upside down." Sylvie starts to laugh and looks in her bag for a mint and holds one in her hand and looks up at the therapist.

"I felt so uncomfortable in the greenroom," she says, "before and after the show. All the other girls were lying around in their underwear, laughing, showing off. I remember thinking they must have thought I was the most awkward person they had ever seen in their lives."

"I'm sure they weren't thinking that," the therapist says. "You were probably very interesting to them as the new girl."

"I wish I had a picture from that time to show you. I was frizzy, spindly, kind of like a human spider. I looked like I was put together wrong."

The therapist smiles. "I bet most of the girls felt similar on the inside at that age."

"I doubt it. They seemed pretty happy with themselves. If any of them felt awkward, they were awkward like the awkward characters in teen dramas, so, I mean, beautiful, and not actually awkward at all."

The therapist smiles.

Sylvie stretches out her legs. "I used to love those teen dramas," she says. "I loved seeing awkward characters from the outside, done in an attractive, acceptable way."

The therapist nods.

"Maybe that's why I like therapy so much. It's your job to try to put me in a good light. You can't let it show if you think I'm an awkward person, a wrong person."

"I don't think you're awkward or wrong," the therapist says.

"But I haven't said everything yet," Sylvie says.

Sylvie feels a block of air coming in front of her like concrete, like a steep slope.

"I keep trying to tell you something," Sylvie says.

The therapist nods a slow nod.

Sylvie sits on her hands, looks down, and breathes out slowly. Something in time seems to be stopping her from saying what she wants to say. Something in time or something that maintains the order of the universe.

"I used to try to get the accessories that the popular girls had," Sylvie says. "I'd ask my mum to buy them for me. Like Head bags. I asked her for a Head bag."

"I don't think I know those," the therapist says, smiling.

"She actually bought me one. They actually let her buy one in Argos. I thought only the mothers of popular girls would be allowed to buy them."

The therapist laughs. "And how did it feel, having a Head bag?"

"It felt really good. I liked using the zip. I liked touching it, it was so soft. But it was still my awkward hands holding it. So I don't think I pulled it off."

"Don't buy into that, don't buy into *pulling something off.* You had the bag as much as anybody else had the bag. Maybe you were trying to get elsewhere by having the bag and maybe getting the bag wasn't the way to get there . . ."

Sylvie plays with her bottom lip.

"But you had the bag and you enjoyed having it, and you were entitled to enjoy it as much as anybody else. I'm glad your mum bought the bag for you."

"I don't know the word to describe what these things signified," Sylvie says. "Head bags and other things: ankle chains, leg warmers. They seemed to possess magic. The girls that had them somehow looked like natural animals with them. Like they were supposed to be where they were, doing what they were doing, making the shapes in the air that they were making."

The therapist looks at Sylvie.

"I'm talking about the popular girls. They had these things, and it's like they were irresistible. It makes me feel sick just thinking about it."

"I think it was your fantasy that these girls looked like *natural animals*," the therapist says. "We don't know what was going on inside their heads, we don't know what they were going through at home."

Sylvie takes a sip of water. "Jade, Rachel, Melanie . . ." she says slowly. Whatever they were going through at home, she would have taken it if it meant she could have been more like them.

"I think you would look natural in leg warmers or an ankle bracelet," the therapist says brightly.

Sylvie starts to blush and dips her head. She pictures herself in Reebok high-tops with leg warmers and an ankle chain and wonders if she could pull it off, now that she's older.

"And we can work on you feeling natural on the inside in therapy."

Sylvie nods slowly, gritting her teeth at *on the inside*. "I feel bad for myself at that age. For how disgusting I felt. I mean, I still feel disgusting now."

"You're not disgusting," the therapist says.

"I keep trying to tell you something," Sylvie says.

Sylvie suddenly feels tired, like someone would have to wind her up for her to be able to say another word. She starts to tug at her bottom lip and she looks up at the therapist and starts to twist her lip on each tug.

"Maybe next week?" the therapist says, and Sylvie looks at her. The sun has come round to the center of the window now, so that Sylvie can see a silhouette of the therapist, and she sees that the therapist looks to be just the same shape as Lady Diana.

4

THE ONE FORM

SYLVIE WALKS HOME trying not to touch parts of her body with other parts of her body—she lifts her arms away from her torso and spreads out her fingers. She feels like her body wants to scream in its desperation to turn back to the therapist's house. She knew this would happen, she knew she would want to turn around and go straight back if she hadn't said what she had decided to say—what she had been dying to tell the therapist every second of last week. But she keeps walking. When she walks past the wall that encloses the therapist's garden, she pictures herself scraping her wrists along it, over the googly-eye graffiti that has always been there, to make the eyes look bloodshot.

At home, Sylvie glances at the evidence of her preparation for therapy—coffee grounds spilled over the kitchen counter, knickers on the bathroom floor, hair straightener turned on in the bedroom. It looks as if she'd been making preparations to try to trick the therapist in some way, as if she'd been getting ready for some kind of performance. Her whole life feels little more than preparation for therapy now, really. Whenever she leaves her house, all her brain is interested in is finding the shape of the therapist. If her eyes see a person from a distance that could fit that shape, her brain tries to believe it's her. As the person gets closer, and Sylvie sees that it is somebody else—a stranger—her brain takes the difference as a distortion, it sees it as grotesque, the way the face stretches or squashes into a different shape, the wrong shape. The chin squashes down, the nose spreads out, the eyes bulge, the body shrinks, grows lumps in different places.

Sylvie gets her phone out of her bag. She feels a rush of something that feels similar to how she thinks happiness feels, when she considers a way of thinking in which it would be fine, normal, for her to text the therapist what she hadn't managed to say in her session. She feels something sparkling, like jellied sweets, come to the surface of her face, as if her body has pushed the good stuff in her up to the top. She opens a new message and types the beginning of the therapist's name. Sylvie breathes in quickly when her phone autofills the rest. Seeing that the therapist's name is there, in her phone, makes Sylvie feel like she has entered a magazine. She starts typing out a message: *All I think about . . .* she types, but then deletes, and starts again with: *As soon as I leave the therapy room . . .* and she stops. She notices her reflection in the phone screen, sees that she looks like Screech from *Saved by the Bell*, and quickly drops her phone.

Sylvie runs herself a bath and takes a packet of Jelly Babies in with her, keeping one hand above water to eat them with. She remembers how she used to swap sweets at the school bus stop with one of the twins. She isn't sure which twin—she'd dated both of them, but had only been able to tell them apart by their hair. Maybe it was the one with the floppier River Phoenix hair, not the one with the back-combed Robert Smith hair, whom she had done it with. Whichever one, he'd asked for a sweet and she'd had one in her mouth, a Kola Cube, and she had kissed him and pushed it into his mouth with her tongue. After that, it became something they did, swapping sweets while kissing. Probably lots of people did it. But not when they get older. She wonders if the therapist would do it. Are things more disgusting when you get older? People's mouths? Sylvie realizes a song is playing in her head, a song she liked when she was twelve or so. *Sugar and spice, everything nice.*

Sylvie stares at the bath taps and wonders if there could be something magical about the composition of the therapist's face. She wants to work out why glimpsing the therapist's face so briefly—in the bright aisles of the supermarket, or at the petrol pump in the rain—makes Sylvie feel like she is living inside sunshine for hours afterward. She starts to chain-eat the sweets, one after the other. Could the therapist's face be better-quality than any other face she's seen? High-quality and rare? A pearl face, a caviar face, a painite face, a truffle face. But she knows it's wrong to think about quality in people. Sylvie tries harder to picture the therapist's face and somehow, like a music video she feels she watched as a child but can't place, the face keeps morphing, from a young girl's face to a man's face, to the face of a teenage boy, then to an older woman. Sylvie lets the pictures change while she lies in the bath, and the same lyrics play in her head, something like *you got it girl with the sugar and spice.* If the therapist's face is ageless and sexless as only the face of a god could be, she thinks, then maybe it's okay to think of it as higher quality than the faces of regular humans.

The air suddenly goes cold and Sylvie turns and sees that the door is open, and her dog, Curtains, is walking in circles on the bath mat. Sylvie leans backward to push the door shut, then fills her mouth with the rest of the sweets. Maybe it's not magic, she thinks, maybe it's an accident. An accident of nature, like Curtains's squashed brain, or like the dog with one eye in Ripley's Believe It or Not! The therapist's face could be, through an accident of nature, a composite of all the faces of the people Sylvie loved the most—her best friend at school, her favorite boyfriend, the choirboy who was always on TV when she was growing up, her high school English teacher, River Phoenix.

Sylvie slides underwater, keeping one arm hanging down over the bath to reassure Curtains. Different lyrics are playing in her head now; she's arrived at the chorus and hears: *We'll believe now in nothing at all, nothing compares with the love of the one form.* Sylvie pictures the poster of the singer that had been above her bed when she was twelve. He'd had a black hat propped on the back of his head so that it looked like a black halo. Without that hat, the singer would have looked a lot like the therapist too. *Nothing compares with the love of the one form,* she thinks, sitting up in the bath. What did he mean? What is the one form? She pulls the sweets bag underwater and watches the sugar dissolve. *Is the therapist the one form, for me?*

5

BODY STORAGE

SYLVIE GETS TO WORK ten minutes early for handover, as she is supposed to. She sees the head vet's long silver car in the parking lot and for a second imagines it will make her go blind, but it doesn't, and she carries on and opens the door to the clinic. Upstairs, she puts her things away. She leaves an empty peg on each side when she hangs up her coat so her coat doesn't touch anyone else's coat, and she puts her lunch away at the back of the fridge so it doesn't touch anyone else's lunch.

There are five patients in the ward, the rest of the cages are empty. The empty cages are lined neatly with newspaper, the stainless steel bars clean and shining. Sylvie wants to give them as much attention as she gives the occupied cages, but she picks up the clipboard and makes notes on the inpatients as the night nurse starts to speak. Who needs repeat bloods, who needs X-rays, who is going home. The night nurse is tall and slim and married, and has a lot of experience.

When the night nurse leaves, Sylvie stands in front of each occupied kennel in turn. She says hello to each patient. She tries to think of ways their names fit their appearance, so she can remember who is who. She does this before the vet comes down, while her brain is free to work. She knows that the vet could come in from one of three doors to get to the ward. Sylvie pins her fob watch to her tunic, checks her scissors, locates the keys for the dangerous drugs. *I am at work*, she thinks. *I'm one of the nurses.*

All day she works hard, but she leaves the phones to the others, imagining there will be trouble and confusion at the end of the line. Instead she does laundry, she folds drapes, she slowly injects drugs into drip lines. If Sylvie is asked to discharge patients, she talks to the client, praising their pet, saying how good they are, how they did really well.

"We need to make sure she doesn't lick the wound," Sylvie says. "The cone needs to stay on at all times."

"She's not going to like that," the owner says.

Sylvie nods and strokes the pet sitting on the table between them.

"We just don't want it to get infected," Sylvie says. "If it gets infected, she might have to come back and get it stitched up again. And we wouldn't want that," Sylvie says, smiling.

The clients smell like cigarettes, Sylvie thinks. They smell of cigarettes and do what they want. They have the air of people who have everything they like stacked up in their living room, on every surface.

While Sylvie cleans the consult room, she wonders what the therapist would be like with a different client. She imagines the air of the therapy room tinged with red, getting murky from the breath and sweat of the other client. She imagines the therapist sliding off her chair, slowly dying from boredom, from the predictability of what she's hearing. Sylvie could come to her front door, press the buzzer, and revive her. She could be a breath of fresh air. When the door is opened, she could kiss the therapist, put her hand on the back of the therapist's head, both their heads tilted at an angle. Would the therapist do that? If her husband let her? Sylvie imagines a small button at the back of the therapist's head that she could press, that would make the therapist's tongue pop out, and with it, the truth about how she feels about Sylvie. The phone rings in the consult room, but Sylvie doesn't answer it. *The phones are everywhere, they ring from everywhere,* she thinks.

The head nurse has put Sylvie on Ops for the afternoon. Sylvie holds a dog for its injection, opens its jaw so the vet can place a tube, works the anesthetic machine. She shaves fur in a neat rectangle, moves sterile swabs outward from the center, carries the dog to the operating theater. She listens to the heartbeats and watches the breaths—counts them every five minutes and fills in the chart. The vet is the one going in, making incisions, taking things out.

"How's she doing?" the vet says.

"Good," Sylvie says.

"Three-metric catgut," the vet says, and Sylvie gets the catgut as quickly as she can, imagining herself a spirit with no body that moves quicker than a body. She offers up the catgut, careful not to touch anything—the vet, the instruments—careful not to break the sterility. The vet lifts the ovaries and uterus into the air and Sylvie offers up a bowl and receives them, then carries on with the chart. There is boredom there, in the air around her, but she is working hard, and the animal is still alive, and nothing has gone wrong, and does anyone exist without boredom? No human brain can have that kind of life, Sylvie thinks. Maybe Kate Moss's brain, and Madonna's, but not many others.

On afternoon break, Sylvie goes to the locker room. There's an envelope in her locker, hidden inside a human first-aid book that she's never had occasion to use. Inside the envelope are pictures of the therapist. Sylvie had only been able to find three images of the therapist online, all from different therapy directories, and she'd printed them out at the pharmacy. She looks inside the envelope, feels a shot of love, and smiles. A vet enters the room and Sylvie quickly puts the envelope in her tunic pocket. She thinks she probably looks like a regular nurse to the vet, one of the shyer ones, but a nurse nonetheless, a nurse who works hard, then goes home to her boyfriend to watch TV. Sylvie decides to go down to the basement, to the body storage. Nobody stays down there longer than they have to, they hold their breath, put the bodies into the chest, and leave, because it's dark, and it's cold, and it smells of death.

Sylvie crouches by the side of a freezer and gets the envelope out. Some of the photos are so pixelated they don't even look like a person. She could call this an art project, if anyone caught her, if anyone asked. Sylvie had wanted to work out which part of the therapist's face was driving her crazy, so she'd moved an image of the therapist around on her phone, taking screenshots of all the different parts. It seemed to be the eyes and the hair. Then she had wanted to work out how small a section of the eyes and the hair could drive her crazy, so she'd zoomed in on these sections, further and further, until her screen showed just the tiniest slice of an eye, the tiniest sliver of hair, and she had taken screenshots and printed them out. She is looking at one of these pictures now, and the effect is strong and immediate. Sylvie's back slides down the body freezer until she is sitting on the floor. Still looking at the pictures, she lets her head fall forward and her mouth opens slightly and she starts to drool. She's stepped into the other dimension, where there is calm and there is certainty and in the certainty there is ecstasy, and for once she is a natural animal, and the world is just as directed, and it is beautiful. Sylvie wipes her mouth, then lifts her fob watch with a quick, assured movement. Its hands are glowing in the dark. She wants to see how long it takes for the effect to wear off.

6

CLEAN BEDSHEET

SYLVIE IS JUST ABOUT TO LEAVE for therapy: she has straightened her hair, brushed her teeth, ironed her shirt. She'd felt breathless all morning, so excited to see the therapist that she didn't think she'd be able to get herself ready, but she got herself ready, running on a lower level of consciousness. She goes quickly to the kitchen to get a pack of mints and steps in a puddle in her socks: Curtains has peed on the floor.

Sylvie pulls her socks off and runs upstairs to get new ones, singing, *Nappies, nappies, nappies*, as she runs, hoping there are more of her favorite socks in the drawer: long, white, ribbed. She thinks about Curtains's puddle, how she needs to clean it up. She'd made a puddle like that at school once, in biology, when she'd been too shy to ask to go to the toilet. She'd felt it run down her legs, into her socks, and onto the floor, and when it finally stopped, she'd walked quickly out of the classroom and locked herself in the toilet. She'd stayed there in the silence, patting her knickers dry with blue paper towels. When she returned, the puddle was no longer there. She'd lifted her gaze from the floor and scanned the room to see if she was being watched, but her classmates kept their eyes down, concentrated on their diagrams, the cross section of an animal cell. Sylvie wonders what the teacher had said to the class to make them stay quiet, wonders how many girls had laughed as they'd watched him clean it up.

It's sunny when Sylvie leaves the house and so she goes back in to get sunglasses, though she's running late already. When she leaves for the second time, she kicks her door hard to shut it. Seeing her black shoe with its white sock at the end of her body, she feels that she's seen something similar in a gallery. The shine of the patent leather and the rib of the white sock, in the sun, create an end-of-school feeling of joy.

As she walks, she can hear the clang of scaffolding poles being erected around somebody's house behind her. Sylvie's hair falls over her sunglasses. She's sucking on a mint, trying to make it last, but when she gets to the white wall that marks the beginning of the therapist's property, she grinds the mint up in less than a second. Sylvie sees the therapist's car parked across the road from the therapist's house and feels terrific luck. She wonders if she is the luckiest person alive in the world at that moment. But of course the car would be there, the therapist is in, Sylvie knows she is in, she is just about to have her session. The car is jet-black and perfect, like a drawing of a car, a shining sticker of a car. Always clean and exactly the same. There seems to be a shield around the car a

few inches thick and white like dry ice that stops Sylvie getting closer, stops her jumping on its bonnet and telling it she
loves it.

Sylvie is at the front door and she presses the buzzer. It's
a circle within many circles and she has to press hard. Sylvie
puts her face up to the glass in the door and waits until the
shape of the therapist comes toward her. Through the thick
curved glass, it looks like she's gliding. Sylvie steps back
quickly and the therapist opens the door, and Sylvie goes up
the stairs, *One, two, three, shake your body down.*

The therapist sits down and crosses her legs. She is wearing white trousers, a white blouse, and a cream cardigan. Sylvie tries to make her gaze look distant and unfocused while
she looks at the therapist's hands. The gold ring is still on the
therapist's middle finger. The ring is thick. Sylvie feels as if
she is taking information from the therapist that she shouldn't
be taking, but the information she is taking is just: *The ring is
still there, and it is thick.*

"How have you been?" the therapist says, smiling.

Sylvie puts her hand in her bag until she finds a mint and
she puts it in her mouth, remembering the promise she made
to herself to get the words out this week.

"Do you remember last session," Sylvie says, "the end
of it?"

"I'm not sure," the therapist says, tilting her head.

"I was trying to tell you something, but I didn't manage,
and you said: *Maybe next week.*"

"Yes," the therapist says, beaming. "I remember. Do you
want to talk about it now?"

"I've been dying to text you about it all week. I kept having to stop myself from texting you."

"And you managed. You were able to wait."

Sylvie starts to play with her bottom lip, squeezing and twisting it. She can tell how little the therapist would have cared to receive a text from her between sessions, outside of the time she was paying for. Had Sylvie been expecting the therapist to say, *That would have been fine, just text next time*?

"But it was really hard," Sylvie says. "I was constantly writing, deleting, writing, deleting, a few times a day. Even at work."

Sylvie looks across at the therapist's lap and remembers always wanting blancmange on her birthday. She loved how it looked, with the red cherry on top, but when she got it, she never ate it. She looks up at the therapist.

"I just wanted to tell you . . . that whenever I leave this room . . ." she says, then stops.

"Yes," the therapist says.

Sylvie stretches her arms out and pulls her cardigan sleeves over her hands. It's happening again, it's becoming physically impossible to say it, but she has to say it, if she doesn't say it, the disappointment, the boredom, the frustration of another week of waiting to say it in the next session will be too much to bear. Her future self makes her do it, makes her say it.

"Whenever I leave this room, I just want to come straight back again."

The therapist nods but doesn't smile, and Sylvie continues.

"I just want to be here all the time," Sylvie says.

She looks over at the thick cream door. Bright sunlight is hitting it and Sylvie sees that the door is made up of two crosses and in the negative space of the crosses are rectangles and she counts the rectangles, there are six, then she says, "I think about you all the time."

The room feels like a stage set and Sylvie feels that she's said her lines, and she hears the therapist say, "I think that's okay for now. It might just mean that the therapy is working."

She looks across at the therapist's face; it looks soft and dry like birthday cake. Sylvie closes her mouth. She had thought her mind had been doing something wrong, repulsive, possibly illegal, but the therapist is acting like what she was reporting was to be expected. She watches the therapist smooth out the creases in her white trousers. Apart from the rhythmic sounds of the therapist's hands, the room is silent. Sylvie feels for a moment that she's in the same body that she's always been in, and the feeling of familiarity isn't boring or cloying, it feels like an achievement to balance through time.

"It's maybe six hundred times a day," Sylvie says, and then she stops and the therapist tilts her head.

"That I think about you," Sylvie goes on, the word *you* said so quietly as to be barely audible.

The therapist's expression doesn't change, and Sylvie smiles at this lack of concern, and stretches her legs out in front of her. The carpet goes on like crushed biscuit. There is a scratching noise and the therapist and Sylvie turn to look at the door.

"It's Butter," the therapist says. "He shouldn't do that, I'm sorry. He shouldn't try to come in."

"I don't mind," Sylvie says.

The therapist stands up and Sylvie sees that she is wearing a cream belt with her white trousers. The therapist's dog, Butter, runs in when she opens the door. Sylvie puts out her hand and when he comes up to her, she strokes him tentatively. She sees that the therapist's dog is a different shape than her own dog, Curtains. His legs are longer and he doesn't have patches on his head or body. The therapist's dog is white all over like a clean bedsheet.

7

MAYBE BOTH

"I DON'T KNOW whether it's . . . transference, or, you know, a crush," Sylvie had said, and the therapist had said gently, "Maybe both."

Sylvie discovered that, at the end of that session, and the end of all sessions from then on, her eyes couldn't focus completely on her walk home. She would feel like she was walking through black-and-white static—a mass of confusion—the war of the ants. She wondered if the static was the only way she could move from the reality in the therapist's room to the reality in her own house. The static would fall away as Sylvie reached her front door and her sight became clear again. And her brain would switch from thinking of her love for the therapist as a fantasy—some combination of transference and a crush—to believing in it again as a reality, a reality that could be acted upon.

Sylvie then could become blissfully happy whenever she pictured her therapist, for the rest of the week. She would feel that she and the therapist were connected, thinking of each other most of the time, maybe without even realizing. They were sitting on the steps of a huge abandoned church, chatting, drinking coffee made with Coffee-mate, psychically speaking. They were lying on a white duvet surrounded by cream cakes, opening books and putting their fingers under the passages that resonated the most, both at the same time. But when Sylvie's next session came round, and she was where she had longed to be all week—in the same room as the therapist—she would straightaway understand that the therapist was a stranger. She wouldn't dream of moving her chair a millimeter closer. Getting out of her chair to touch the person who all week she had considered her soul mate was unthinkable. Sylvie would stay in the patient's chair, the chair that'd had another patient sitting in it maybe just eleven minutes earlier. The therapist wouldn't have been thinking about Sylvie all week, looking forward to their next session. She would have been busy, kissing her husband, maybe on a yacht, drinking white wine with their mutual friends, interesting and successful.

Sometimes this setup seemed good to Sylvie. She was paying for fifty minutes with the therapist, and even with all the time she spent staring at her shoes or the window or the small clock, she felt she saw enough beauty in the session to sustain her for the rest of the week. Therapy gave Sylvie the feeling that she was being looked after and thought about every minute of every hour outside of therapy too. It was only during the fifty minutes when she was actually being thought about and looked after that she realized this wasn't the case. Sometimes this seemed lucky, but sometimes, when Sylvie looked in the mirror to brush her hair, she thought to herself: *What kind of torture is this, the way dwelling in fantasy and reality alternate and never once believe in each other?*

8

A WAX MODEL

THE THERAPIST ASKS if Sylvie is *dating at the moment* and Sylvie can't believe her ears. Does the therapist think Sylvie is walking around like a regular person, looking at other regular people and working out which one she wants to get undressed next to, which one she wants to rub her private bits onto? Does the therapist think this is where she is at, in terms of being human? And does she even remember last session? Did she not hear how complete Sylvie's obsession with her is? Her emotions are all with the therapist, there's nothing left for anyone else.

"Have you thought about what kind of person you'd like to meet?" the therapist says.

"There isn't a kind of person I'd like to meet," Sylvie says. "I don't even know if I'd be looking for a man or a woman.

I have no criteria. The only time I take an interest in another person at the moment is if they look, you know . . ."

"No, I don't know," the therapist says, smiling.

Sylvie scowls at having to say it aloud. "If they look like you."

They both laugh a short laugh, then Sylvie lowers her head and when she sees her legs, it doesn't seem right to her to see them there, with socks and shoes. *I'm a person*, she thinks, *a person with a body, who has got their body out of bed and dressed it in clothes and shoes and taken it to meet another person.* She wonders if she can carry on with the conversation now that she's noticed, but doesn't really see another option.

"I know it's unlikely that will happen," she says.

The light behind the therapist is especially bright today, which makes it hard for Sylvie to see her face. Sylvie wonders if the therapist has set up the chairs like this on purpose so she can run the session with a halo.

"I wonder what it would be like, though, if I did find someone who looked like you."

"I think it would depend on what the person was like," the therapist says.

"Maybe whatever they were like, I'd get a core feeling of happiness. You don't know what's going on inside a person anyway, so if they *look like* a person you like, maybe that would be enough."

"I think you can get to know what's going on inside a person over time."

"I went out with this man at college once because he looked like a writer I liked, a crime writer."

The therapist nods.

"The writer had such a good look. I had a picture of him up in my room in halls. And then I noticed this mature student around college that reminded me of him. I think it was his mustache. He had a similar mustache."

Sylvie looks at the therapist and blushes, feeling guilty for mentioning mustaches when there seems something deviant about liking them, and when the therapist could never have one herself.

"I went up to him one time when I was having a really boring day. I think the boredom overpowered my shyness. I asked him if he wanted to go for coffee. He said no at first but then he changed his mind. And we kind of started seeing each other. He was sleeping on his friend's sofa in a council flat near Baker Street and we used to get food and hang out there. I remember one time we went to a shitty supermarket by the station and he told me to get whatever I wanted and I chose a slab of angel cake, that pink and yellow cake. I think that gave him a hard-on."

The therapist twists her ring around her finger. "How old was he?"

"I think he was fifty. He told me he was fifty."

"And did you feel that he was enough like the crime writer?"

"I suppose I didn't know what the crime writer was like. It's the same with you, I don't know what you're like when you're not working."

"I'm not that different than how I am when I'm working."

Sylvie looks at the therapist. She tries to imagine talking to the therapist against a different background, maybe standing up, the therapist's face and body not at work. The room looks so insistently itself suddenly, and Sylvie stops trying, looks at her feet, tries to remember what she had been talking about.

"It was fun at first, or at least interesting. He would have me do things like stand in the corner of the room and lift up my slip. I was wearing slips at the time because the characters in the crime writer's books wore slips."

The therapist frowns and nods.

"But then we were messing around on the sofa one time and it was really dark, though it was just the afternoon. The curtains were closed, they were really thick, and *Gladiators* was on in the background. He was trying to find out if I was a virgin—I mean by asking me. There was some confusion, maybe I mumbled, or didn't want him to know, and he got excited, he thought the plan was that he was going to take my virginity, and I suddenly wanted to leave. I got up and straightened myself out, but he slipped in front of me and put his hand on the front door and quickly locked it."

Sylvie's mouth goes dry and she moves her tongue around before she speaks. "I remember thinking: *Oh, this is actually happening.*"

The therapist frowns and nods.

"His face was red. After a few minutes his expression changed. He laughed, pretended he'd been joking, unlocked the door, and I ran out. I followed the concrete path and just concentrated on finding my way out of the estate."

"Did you see him again after that?"

"I saw him in the college library one time. He came up to me and apologized. Then he said he'd been thinking of getting me a puppy. He said if I went round to his flat every day to look after it, he'd buy me one. He was whispering because we were in the library."

"A puppy?"

"I know!" Sylvie laughs and shakes her head. "I suppose dating a look-alike is a bit like going to Madame Tussauds," she says.

The therapist tilts her head.

"The wax museum," Sylvie says. "You go and see waxworks of famous people and get your picture taken with them. Kate Moss, Madonna, Michael Jackson. It's a really stupid day out."

"I suppose it's supposed to be lighthearted," the therapist says.

"Imagine if they weren't waxworks, that would be stressful. If all those famous people were all in one room, and you were there too."

The therapist smiles. "But when you're dating a look-alike, you're not dating a wax model. It's a real person. And it can be dangerous to project your feelings for somebody else onto them, onto a stranger, as you found out with this mature student, this look-alike of the crime writer."

Sylvie nods. "And I did the same thing with actual boyfriends. I did the same thing when me and Sandy split up."

"What did you do?"

"I tried to find a Sandy look-alike. It took a few years, but finally I met Owen, and he looked pretty similar to Sandy, so I asked him out."

"I didn't know that's why you went out with Owen," the therapist says. "I didn't know Owen looked like Sandy."

Sylvie nods. "But he wasn't anything like Sandy. Owen

was pretty much the complete opposite of Sandy, on the inside. Sandy was really easygoing, he didn't care what I did, I mean he liked it when I went to parties without him, had fun and sent him pictures. But you know how uptight Owen was, how he policed everything I did. He'd even check through the books I read, before I read them, to see if he thought they were suitable."

The therapist nods and frowns.

"Owen had only read one book in his entire life. But Sandy worked in a bookshop! Sandy never *stopped* reading."

"Owen had read one book?" the therapist says. "What was the book?"

"*The Terminator*. A novelization of the film." Sylvie makes an incredulous face. "I can't believe I let him go through my books like that."

"Well, you can learn from what happened. There's a pattern here. You go for the look-alikes, trying to find something you've lost, or something you feel you can't have. Recognizing a pattern like this can be the first step to changing your behavior. You can make a different decision next time."

Sylvie nods. "Don't expect to get what you want when you go for the look-alikes."

The therapist looks at Sylvie, smooths her hair down with one hand, and smiles.

"The experience with the *actual* crime writer was bad too, though, but in a different way," Sylvie says.

"You met the crime writer? And something happened?"

Sylvie blushes. She doesn't want the therapist to think she falls for people out of reach often, she doesn't want her crush on the therapist to be seen as just another crush in a string of crushes. "I went to one of his readings and gave him a drawing I'd done of his dog."

"That sounds nice," the therapist says.

"He seemed really happy with it," Sylvie says. "He said he was just about to get another dog, a female, and that he'd name it after me."

"How nice. And did he?"

"I don't think so. I don't know. He promised me other things—he said he'd send me all his books, signed with his dog's paw print. I spent pretty much a whole year waiting for that parcel of books, I could think of nothing else. But it never came."

"Oh, you must have been disappointed."

"He probably started to worry that I was obsessed," Sylvie says. "He probably thought it was dangerous to encourage me."

"He may have just been busy. He was a successful writer. There could have been lots of reasons he didn't get around to sending the parcel, reasons that had nothing to do with what he thought of you."

"I wanted that package so much. I still have dreams where I go back to halls and look for it in all the pigeonholes in case it was put in the wrong one. All these years later."

The therapist smiles.

"But I didn't want anything from the look-alike," Sylvie says, "when it actually came to it. I didn't want sex, and I didn't want a real-life puppy from the look-alike, when it actually came to it."

The therapist frowns and nods and then her eyes move to the clock on the mantelpiece.

"I had this awful recurring nightmare when I was little," Sylvie says then, talking quickly. "I'd just been swimming, and I'd come out of the changing rooms and run up to my mum, but she'd be strange, a bit quiet with me, and I'd look around, and see another woman who looked just like my mum standing somewhere else, so I'd run up to her, and hold her hand, but she wasn't quite right either. Then I'd get scared, I'd look all around, and every adult there had my mum's face and my mum's body, and I didn't know which was my real mum, and I didn't know how to find out."

9

SEPARATE BRAIN

SYLVIE PUTS HER THERAPY FOLDER ON HER LAP and opens it to the last page. Curtains is walking in circles, making clicking noises on the wood floor that sound like, *I won't I won't I won't.* Sylvie scans the floor for puddles or wet footprints and, seeing none, picks Curtains up and sets her on the sofa. She watches the dog's eyes cross. "Don't go to the toilet," she says, "not on the sofa." Sylvie strokes Curtains's forehead, thinks about the insides of her, how she has all the same machinery as Sylvie, more or less. Bladder, kidneys, liver, stomach, heart—they're all doing the same job inside Curtains as they're doing inside her. The organs are doing so much work it makes Sylvie feel like laughing. Could it be worth it, doing all that work? But if it isn't worth it in Curtains, then it isn't worth it in her either, she thinks. Sylvie flicks through her therapy folder, skims the last page of notes to see if she covered everything she wanted to cover last session. She finds something she'd forgotten to tell the therapist and writes it out on a fresh page, puts a star next to it.

It concerned a poster she'd put up when she was with Owen. It was a poster of the cover of a book Sylvie liked that had a line drawing of a monster in the center. Sylvie still has the book—it hadn't been in the pile of books Owen had told her to get rid of, though she's sure the book had some sex scenes in it. Owen had probably missed them, maybe he'd gone through it too quickly. Or maybe he had liked the story, Sylvie thinks, starting to feel sick. Maybe he'd wanted her to keep that book because the boy controls the girl in the story, the brother was the one making up all the rules of the "Game." Sylvie had put the poster up in the landing next to their bedroom, but seeing it reflected in the mirror one morning, she'd realized it was an *ambiguous image*—a drawing that can be seen in two different ways. The second image was one of two people kissing. Sylvie knew she had to stop Owen from seeing the kissing image when he looked at it but she couldn't control how his eyes would see it, she couldn't control his brain. She just had to hope that he would always see the monster or he would think her a pervert, tell her to take it down, get rid of it.

Sylvie puts Curtains back on the floor and the dog starts to circle. Curtains's eyes look more like human eyes than dog eyes to Sylvie. Blue-gray, watery, they look a lot like her dad's eyes, at least how they started to look as he got increasingly sick. Sylvie lets herself imagine for a moment that her dad is there, inside Curtains's body, checking in on her. Maybe it was easier to go into the head of an animal that was brain-damaged, maybe the damage gave a bit of space, some kind of open channel. Sylvie remembers the last conversation she'd had with her dad, when she'd gone to see him in the morgue. It had been a one-way conversation, but it had been good, and she'd felt understood. Sylvie watches Curtains move her body around the room—the way she moves her shoulders up with effort reminds her of Quasimodo. *Could* her dad be in there? Watching her write her notes? He wouldn't approve of her going to therapy, she's pretty sure of that; he'd think it ridiculous, self-absorbed. Sylvie closes the folder, Curtains keeps circling. If she really thought her dad was in there, wouldn't she start talking to him? Feed him better-quality chicken, sing him his favorite song? Sylvie leans down and puts a hand out to calm Curtains, stop her from circling. "*Help*," she whisper-sings, "*I need somebody, help, not just anybody.*" Curtains keeps staring into space, and Sylvie carries her to the kitchen. "*Sanctuary!*" Sylvie shouts when she puts the dog down gently on her bed.

Sylvie drives to the supermarket and in the aisles, she looks for peach milk without knowing why. *Does peach milk exist?* Should she ask someone? She can imagine peach milk but can't find any. Sylvie walks up and down each aisle, all the time looking out for the therapist, and in the second-to-last aisle spots a white bottle with a picture of a peach, but it's alcohol, not milk, she's in the alcohol aisle. She starts to walk faster, but she stops at a screen—it's CCTV, she sees herself there. She moves her head around, tries to see herself from different angles. She looks exactly the same as she looked when she was with Sandy, she concludes happily. Before she even *met* Owen. A worker, in an orange polo top and trousers, smiles at Sylvie watching herself, says, "Looking good!" Sylvie blushes, starts to panic, remembering what Owen had said to her once. She types it into her phone so she'll remember it to tell the therapist next session. *When you're somewhere without me, imagine that I'm with you at all times so you won't say anything inappropriate.*

Sylvie buys a multipack of mints on her way out. When she walks through the parking lot, she looks out for the therapist's car, though she doubts it will be there. Knowing she'll have to wait until next week to tell the therapist what she just remembered about Owen, she pictures the week ahead as a long unspeaking gray lump, made of something fatty, that she wants to disappear. The hours at work, she'll be able to get through because the vet will be telling her what to do every minute. The hours at home, she's not so sure. Sometimes even a minute can feel like agony to get through because of its beating lack, lack of the therapist. She'll have to try to read some of her therapy books. She wants to find cases where the patient is obsessed with their therapist, she wants to see what happens. If the therapist goes over the boundary to satisfy the client's longing, she might buy a copy for the therapist. Then she'll be able to read the book again and imagine the therapist reading it at the same time, but in her separate house, in her separate bed, with her separate brain.

10

ORDINARY THINGS

THE THERAPIST IS WEARING BLACK TROUSERS and a white blouse. This is Sylvie's favorite combination, and it is what Sylvie is wearing this week and it is what she wears every week, it is the only thing she ever wears. Sylvie didn't want this to happen, she didn't want the therapist to wear her favorite outfit in case it made the obsession worse. Sylvie sees that the therapist's blouse has a bow on it, and Sylvie never wears a bow, she doesn't feel that she could pull off a bow, or that she deserves one, and she thinks this difference makes it just about okay. The therapist doesn't look self-conscious about their matching outfits, which makes Sylvie think it wasn't intentional, that it was just one of the therapist's many outfits and this was bound to happen at some point if Sylvie wore the same outfit every week. The therapist looks really good in this outfit, but anyone half decent looks good in this outfit, Sylvie thinks. The therapist puts a glass of water on the table next to Sylvie, and Sylvie wonders if the therapist knows how good she looks in this outfit and hopes she doesn't; she doesn't want the therapist to wear it all the time, and give more fuel to the obsession.

"How have you been?" the therapist says, smiling.

"Good," Sylvie says. "I've just been . . . I've been looking forward to . . . therapy."

"That's nice." The therapist smiles.

"I just wish I'd started sooner. I don't understand why I didn't try therapy before, when things started to go wrong with Sandy. So in my twenties, I guess. Or even before that."

"Well, you might not have been receptive to therapy when you were younger."

Sylvie pictures her past years of unhappiness then like a huge pile of waste—slippery red anatomical waste that she has now to clean up, find the right kind of bag for, label right so the waste truck accepts it.

"When do you think you would have first wanted to come?" the therapist says.

"When I started feeling that something was missing from me, I guess," Sylvie says. "When I felt like I wasn't really a person."

"Do you remember the first time you had that thought, or that feeling?"

"I don't think so. I do remember the first time I spoke to somebody about it, though."

The therapist nods and tilts her head.

"It was to my boyfriend when I was sixteen—my boyfriend

before Nick. We all called him Hatstand. I was visiting Hatstand at the petrol station where he worked. I remember he was in a really good mood, he must have taken something. His eyes were bright, he was swiveling on his chair and tapping nonstop on the white counter. He started talking about this girl we both knew, and when he said her name, I was struck by how it instantly conjured up her personality. I hated hearing him say her name. Because I felt like that kind of conjuring would never happen when somebody said mine."

The therapist nods.

"And that's when I asked Hatstand if he thought there was something missing in me, compared to other girls."

"And what did he say?"

"He didn't say anything. He just scoffed. I suppose the scoff was supposed to mean, *That's something you'd expect to hear from somebody who isn't a real person, someone with something missing from them.*"

The therapist smiles. "Well, you said you thought he had taken drugs. Maybe he just wasn't in the right frame of mind to talk about anything serious."

"Maybe," Sylvie says. She imagines Hatstand telling her what she wanted to hear—that she didn't have anything missing, that she's Sylvie, a great personality. He could have done it, he just didn't want to.

"I think a lot of people that age would feel similar if they were honest with themselves, that they had something missing, that they were lacking something in some way," the therapist says.

"It's just, I never stopped feeling like that. I still feel like that now."

"Tell me how it feels now."

Sylvie looks at the therapist. "If I see someone, say if I see someone walking past my window, my brain will think, *There's a person, going from A to B for a reason, sure they know that B is better. And I wonder how they know. I don't feel that I would know, or walk with such certainty.* I feel like I'm just a set of controls, waiting for a person with certainty to come and work them."

"But you often go from A to B yourself, without anyone instructing you. You go to your job, and you work with a lot of purpose at your job."

Sylvie nods. "I guess I feel like that's not me, in my green tunic. I feel maybe like I'm acting, and I think the other nurses think I'm acting too. I don't fit in."

"I think a lot of people feel they are acting to some extent at work. Maybe you feel it more because you came to that job a bit later; you started when you turned thirty, yes?"

Sylvie nods. "Maybe that's it," she says.

"I think it was brave of you to change careers like that. And you enjoy your job now, you like working with animals."

Sylvie smiles. "I love working with animals. And I like the work, physically. I like taking blood, shaving neat rectangles, injecting meds, filling in charts."

The therapist smiles. Sylvie hopes the therapist likes how she's a nurse, she hopes she finds it sweet and attractive, not boring, unremarkable, or beneath both of their stations. She does feel more authentic working at the vet clinic than she did working in the bookshop in her twenties, though she was accepted more readily by her colleagues at the bookshop.

"It's *outside* of work that's the problem. The only time I see the point in doing anything, outside of work, is when I have therapy to come to. When my house is A and the therapy room is B."

The therapist smiles. "That might be enough for you, for now," she says.

"I'm like a zombie when I come to therapy. I'd be completely unable *not* to come. I'm like this." Sylvie widens her eyes and puts her head on its side, sticks her tongue out the side of her mouth.

The therapist laughs. "Well, I'm glad you come every week. You didn't have anyone to talk to when you were with Owen. He made sure he kept you very isolated."

Sylvie nods and rubs her arms. "I couldn't bear to stop coming to therapy."

"We aren't stopping," the therapist says.

"I'd just rather die than stop."

The therapist looks at her.

"I'd rather kill myself than stop therapy," she says.

"You won't always feel like that," the therapist says after a slight pause.

Sylvie takes a mint from her bag. She hears the therapist's dog bark. Sylvie watches the therapist cross her legs and wonders if she's scared her, wonders if the therapist is thinking it's time to hand Sylvie over to somebody else, another therapist, an institution.

"Shall we talk about things you enjoyed doing, things you saw the point in doing before you met Owen? Because I think Owen stopped you from doing a lot of things you felt natural doing. Maybe you just haven't found your way back to those things yet."

Sylvie looks at the therapist's long peach-colored hair fall-ing down over her perfect outfit and thinks there's nothing else she'd rather look at. "Owen stopped me from doing basi-cally everything, apart from texting him, having sex with him, and making up pet names for him," she says quickly.

The therapist shakes her head slowly and makes eye con-tact with Sylvie and Sylvie holds it and they are both silent for a moment and Sylvie breathes in quickly then looks away.

"The thing is, though, I didn't have much of an idea of myself when I met Owen. The only thing I cared about then was drinking. That's probably why he got away with it—I was pretty much primed for being a puppet, an empty puppet he could put his hand up into."

The therapist frowns and nods.

"Maybe I just never recovered after me and Sandy split up. I felt like a person then, I think. Me and Sandy used to work on our notebooks in the evenings, and we made these little zines. They must have been filled with *something*. So I couldn't have been so empty then."

"That sounds fun. Did you keep any of the zines?" the therapist says.

Sylvie shakes her head. "Owen made me throw them away," she says. "*Made me*," she repeats, mocking herself.

The therapist smiles sadly.

"But after Sandy, I did sometimes write these lists to try to work out what I liked doing, and I remember them. There was a column of things I thought I *should* enjoy, and a column of things I *actually* enjoyed."

"That sounds like a good exercise," the therapist says. "What did you put in each column?"

"Under things I thought I should enjoy, I think I put *parties, going to the pub, going out for meals,*" Sylvie says, grimacing. "*Shopping, watching TV.* I didn't bother putting the things nobody really enjoys, like *seeing family, Christmas, birthdays.*"

"I think some people enjoy those things," the therapist says. "And what about the list of things you actually enjoy?"

"I know I put *kissing* on there. I still agree with that one," she says, blushing. "*Drinking Coke* and *eating fries, eating birthday cake.* They would still be on there too. I think the other things were really specific, like *hitting a piñata when the sweets fall out.*"

"But not at a party," the therapist says.

Sylvie laughs. "Right. Hitting piñatas and eating birthday cake, by myself, not at a party."

The therapist smiles.

"I know there were things on there that I wouldn't put anymore, like *drinking hot milk on my knees, eating meat off the bone.* They seem a bit . . . desperate. Then there was *having Chinese takeaway in the back of a car in a sleeping bag at night.* I assume I must have done that as a child, as it seems so specific, like a memory."

"It is very specific," the therapist says. "It sounds nice."

"I'm keeping that one as a special treat, for the future."

The therapist smiles. "We could also think about the times you've felt like a person even though you haven't been enjoying yourself. The two don't always go together: being a person doesn't necessarily mean enjoying yourself."

Sylvie sighs. She bets the therapist is good at enjoying herself. She bets she does it easily, like everyone else. *What do you enjoy? Food, sex, socializing, travel.*

"It's important to feel you're being genuine," the therapist says, "but you can be genuine when you aren't enjoying yourself."

"But if you're enjoying yourself, and you feel like a person, you feel glad to be a person," Sylvie says. "I do feel like a person when I'm crying, but I don't feel glad about it, I want to end my personhood then, even if I've just found it."

Sylvie looks at the therapist, thinks she looks tired, and wants to make her feel better.

"I had this idea once," she says, "about how I could see myself more as a person. I could video myself doing ordinary things. Getting in the car, getting dressed, buying a coffee. And, watching it back, I would be able to see instantly that I'm a person, just like everybody else."

The therapist nods. "Because you would be seeing yourself from the outside. The same way you see other people."

"Exactly. It's hard when you see other people from the outside but you only know yourself from the inside. It's so hard to compare."

The therapist nods.

"I guess you see parts of yourself every now and then," Sylvie says. "Your feet, your hands, but . . . never the head."

The therapist smiles.

"I always think about this film," Sylvie says, "where a woman is taking off this man's clothes, I think they're both drunk, and he says to her, *If you cut off my head, would I say 'me and my head' or 'me and my body'?*"

"And what did he decide? Or what would *you* say?"

"I'd say *me and my body*. Definitely. He says that too. And then he says: *What right has my head to call itself me?*"

The therapist nods. "What about looking at yourself in the mirror? Would that have a similar effect to videoing yourself?"

"No," Sylvie says. "I hate seeing my reflection in a mirror, alive and thinking in real time. I guess I don't mind as much if I see myself from the side or from the back, say, in a changing room."

"I know what you mean," the therapist says.

"I guess the difference is that in a video, you're seeing yourself doing something in the past," Sylvie says. "So it's easy, like watching other people is easy."

The therapist nods. "But it's not easy, being a human," she says. "I don't think anyone finds it easy."

Sylvie looks at the therapist. She is sure some people find it easy, the people who go to the gym, put time aside to apply makeup, take photos of themselves smiling, for instance.

"Something else you could try," the therapist says, "to feel grounded, to feel like a person, is . . . you could practice mindfulness. You think about where you are and what you're doing. For instance, if you were chopping vegetables, you could think: *It's Saturday night, I'm in my kitchen, the window is open, and I'm chopping vegetables.*"

Sylvie looks out of the window. "I'd like to see a video of therapy. That would be good."

The therapist smiles.

"It would be so nice to have it to watch back. During the 167 hours I'm not at therapy."

The therapist laughs.

"The 167 hours and ten minutes per week that I'm not at therapy."

"Is that what it is?" the therapist says. "You have worked it out exactly."

Sylvie smiles. She bets none of the therapist's other clients have worked it out exactly. She must have done the calculation ten times to check it was right, it didn't seem a high enough number; the time between sessions felt much longer. "If you videoed it so I could watch it back, I could see myself as a person, and also I could have each session a second time. It's easier to take it in properly the second time."

"Do you feel like you don't take it in? What about if you made notes after a session when you got home?"

"I do that already. But I probably forget so much by the time I get home."

The therapist smiles.

"I'd like to see videos of your other sessions too. With your other clients."

"Oh yes?" the therapist says. "I mean, of course that wouldn't be possible. But I'm interested in why you would want to do that."

"I'd like to see how you talk to your other clients, maybe to see if you are the same with them, and if you say the same thing to everybody."

The therapist nods. "I can tell you that I don't say the same thing to everybody."

"Maybe I want to see if you like them more than you like me," Sylvie says, "and see if you look like you're enjoying yourself more, with your other clients."

11

DEATH JUICE

THE CLINIC IS BUSY, Sylvie has been running bloods on all three machines, and when there is a lull, the head nurse tells her to take her break. She goes upstairs, gets her meal deal out of the fridge and her book out of her bag, then heads to the far table, smiling quickly at the two nurses sitting on the big sofa. The nurses are talking about a reality TV show, talking about who they want to stay and who they want to leave. Sylvie keeps her book on her knee while she eats, stares silently at the title on the cover: *Every Day Gets a Little Closer: A Twice-Told Therapy*. She thinks about how the book first came to be—a young woman suffering from writer's block being given therapy in exchange for writing about her sessions afterward, her therapist hoping it would encourage her writing. *Unbelievable*. She's read the whole thing and she hates the ending, hates the patient's afterword, where she reveals she's both *stopped suffering* and she has a *new man* in the same sentence. Sylvie flicks to the end of the book with one hand and reads: *I really find myself feeling more like a woman and less like a girl*, grimaces, and glances over at the nurses.

The nurse with black hair is telling the nurse with red hair about her dinner, then about her boyfriend, and where they are going on holiday. When she stops, the nurse with red hair talks about her dinner, and her boyfriend, and where they are going on holiday, and Sylvie listens, trying not to stare. The door opens quickly and a vet sticks her head round, looking for a nurse. "Can someone help me with a PTS?" she says.

Sylvie raises her hand, then lowers it quickly and gets up, embarrassed, and the vet smiles. The vet says quietly, as Sylvie walks over, "Everything's ready, I just need you to hold," and Sylvie nods gravely.

The old dog is lying on top of a gray towel on the consult room table. Sylvie scans the papers by the computer for the dog's name and sex before she approaches. She strokes the dog, looks up at the owner—an old man—and says the dog is so sweet, calling her by her name, Purdy. When Sylvie sees the vet is ready, she moves to the side of the dog, cradles her head, extends a front leg, and raises the vein with her thumb. The vet checks that the owner is ready, then inserts the needle and slowly depresses the plunger of the syringe. Sylvie keeps her hand holding the dog's leg very still, but her hand holding the head makes regular strokes in the fur. The owner is stroking the fur too, farther down. Sylvie says: "Good dog, good dog, good dog," quietly as she strokes. When the dog stops holding her own body up, Sylvie takes the weight, lowers the head, helps the body lie on its side. All three people look down at the body in silence for a second. The vet moves her stethoscope around the dog's chest, checking for a heartbeat, and when there is none, says quietly, "She's gone, we'll give you some time." Sylvie takes the used syringe and leaves with the vet by the back door, shutting it slowly and quietly behind her. She exhales, and the vet nods, and Sylvie moves across the room and puts the needle in the sharps bin and looks at the pink liquid left in the syringe, thinking, *Death juice.* Then, on tiptoes, she pulls a bag and cable tie down from the top shelf, medium-sized. She's glad the owner wanted time alone, she's glad he wanted to stay. She looks back at the closed door and wonders what's happening in there now, wonders whether anything is happening with the spirit, whether it's going to go out the front door with the owner when he leaves. Would the spirit go home with the owner, even if the body stays at the clinic? Sylvie doesn't think Purdy will come with her, down to the basement when she puts the body in the freezer. She doesn't think any of the animals come down with her, though she always keeps her mouth closed when she's carrying them, just to be on the safe side.

Sylvie goes straight upstairs to finish her lunch after filing the paperwork. She wishes she'd brought a novel to read, not this therapy book—she can't help but compare herself to the patient, Ginny, unfavorably: Sylvie isn't getting the same preferential treatment that Ginny is getting, not by a long shot. Ginny's probably dead now, Sylvie thinks happily, after checking the date of publication and seeing the book came out before she was even born. It happened in a different time.

After break she's put on wards, and Neo, the big dog in the

low kennel, is whining and nudging the bars. Sylvie lifts the stainless steel latch and puts him on a leash, scanning the notes on his kennel before she takes him out. Suspected brucellosis. She googles it while walking the dog around the backyard. It's contagious, it's zoonotic, she checks the symptoms, starts to feel sick, wishes she'd worn gloves. Didn't she do this dog's bloods earlier, package them up for the lab?

She puts Neo back in his kennel and starts to scrub her hands with pink skin wash. As she scrubs, she thinks about the reason she likes her patients: they're cute, and she can't catch anything from them . . . usually. She only wants to see illness and death where she can handle it, where it's no threat to her. And it does seem a bonus that the animals don't speak to ask why they aren't getting better. They can be put to sleep if they are in great pain, if there is no cure. Funny how a nurse for humans is the last job she'd want to do. She couldn't bear to be around human suffering and have to listen to them talking about it. Being a vet nurse is good, Sylvie thinks, drying her hands, then spraying them with alcohol.

12

OUT MORBIDITY

IT IS SATURDAY and Sylvie is sitting on her sofa. Ten minutes ago, she pulled up her blinds and saw the therapist's car pass her house. Sylvie finds this the hardest way of seeing the therapist—driving past in her car. The shining black perfection of the car, the therapist in the driver's seat, not smiling, the perfect shape of her sunglasses, her hair framing both sides of her face. The hands that, in the therapy room, would be bringing Sylvie a glass of water, now on top of the steering wheel, not stopping for her, but passing. Sylvie supposes the therapist is on her way to a friend's house, maybe a photographer for a magazine. They will have cocktails on a balcony, look at the view, and give each other looks that mean, *We are both on the next level.*

Sylvie puts a book in her bag and leaves the house with

Curtains, drives to the beach. It's sunny, then cloudy, then sunny again, and it continues to alternate between the two. Curtains keeps pulling on the leash, trying to get to other places, but Sylvie wants to stay still. She isn't feeling happy, but what proportion of people are feeling happy? Sylvie thinks about the Saturdays she spent in London, going for walks along cracked pavements, past solid buildings with silver tea sets inside, maybe by London Zoo, in cold bright air. She sometimes felt so happy that if something good happened, if she found money or got a text from someone she really liked, Sylvie would panic that things were too good. She worried that something bad would happen to her brain if it got any happier, so she calmed herself by thinking of all the good things that had happened to Kate Moss—this seemed to put the good things that were happening to her into perspective. When she'd told her friend Conrad about this tactic of hers, he'd laughed and said, *Kate Moss is probably a very unhappy person.*

Sylvie looks down at her book, then up again at the sea. This day feels extra, like more than she needs. She's already had so many more days alive than Nick, and Nick had a better brain, and many more ideas than her, about what to do. She tries to read another sentence, then looks up again, thinking about all the different phases she has been through in the many years she's been alive. It disgusts her, all the different things she's tried. Some of them were nice: buying X-Girl clothes, watching skateboarders, trying to skateboard, trying to form a band. It's good to try things, the therapist is always saying this, and people work out who they are by trial and error. But trial and error is messy, and some of the things

Sylvie tried were awful, and she doesn't understand why it seemed okay at the time to try those things. Had she looked at bad things so many times that she didn't recognize that they were bad anymore? Sylvie wishes it could just be the current moment, so the only version of herself that existed was the version she was now. Sylvie watches Curtains digging a hole in the pebbles to curl up in. If she were a dog, she would understand that the current moment is all there is, she thinks.

A woman seems to be approaching Sylvie, making her way across the pebbles. Her hair is brown and shiny and Sylvie gets the feeling of seeing a prefect at boarding school, and feels glad she has a book in her hand. Sylvie smooths her hair down and then the woman is in front of her, saying hello.

"Did I see you at the book club in the library?" the woman says. "Was it you who disappeared in the break?"

Sylvie nods and smiles. "I didn't actually mean to leave," she says. "I just got up and kept walking, and then I was home."

The woman is wearing black shorts and a white blouse and she has a gold ring with a set pearl on her middle finger. Her legs are tanned. She crouches next to Sylvie and picks up a pebble and moves it from hand to hand.

"I wanted to leave too," she says, "but I didn't know how."

They both smile, tell each other their names. Sylvie blushes, and the woman, who is called Chloe, looks at the book on Sylvie's lap.

"I've been meaning to read that book for ages," Chloe says.

"I bought it recently for someone I like," Sylvie says, "so

I'm rereading it, to see if it was appropriate to give it to her. And it really wasn't."

Chloe laughs and picks up the book and starts reading and Sylvie looks at the sea. She tries to stop herself from smiling. It seems too good to be true that someone she's just met is comfortable enough in her presence to be able to read.

"I see what you mean," Chloe says, after reading the first page. "But it's appropriate for me. If you'd given it to me, it would have been appropriate."

Sylvie blushes and smiles. Before she leaves, Chloe asks for Sylvie's number and Sylvie writes it on a pebble with black marker, and Chloe puts the pebble in her pocket.

That evening Sylvie gets a text from Chloe with a link to a video that had just been in a show she'd curated. There are concrete bridges and tarmac roads, it's dark and gray, and somebody is shouting something that sounds like a spell.

I love it, Sylvie messages Chloe, just before the video ends.

Then we can definitely be friends! Chloe says, with a winking emoji.

Out morbidity! Sylvie texts, quoting the video.

It works as an exorcism, Chloe says. *I used it once.*

Maybe I'll use it one day too, Sylvie says.

Useful Art! Chloe says.

When do you want to meet? Sylvie says.

Soon, Chloe says, *and for the rest of your life.*

13

ALL DOGS ARE NICE

THE THERAPIST IS WEARING A WHITE BLOUSE and dark blue jeans which Sylvie thinks are in the cut of *boyfriend* jeans.

"I don't know if there's anything worse than the only person you want not wanting you back," Sylvie says. She's telling the therapist about Sandy, her boyfriend when she was twenty-three and lived in London—the boyfriend she'd wanted to marry.

The therapist nods. Her hair is in a ponytail.

"I sat in my tiny bedroom in Archway doing nothing but crying for weeks after we split up. I wanted that to be the last thing I ever did—crying for Sandy on the floor. I remember thinking the floorboards were getting soft, and I kept picturing a new tenant opening the door and seeing a mound of gray pulp in the middle of the room and wondering what it was, and it would be me and the floorboards, mixed into pulp."

The therapist makes a face and pushes back a stray hair.

"We talked about our breakup when we got back in touch. Sandy said he went down a hole too. I was surprised. I thought he'd just be at the 333, this club we went to, the place we met."

"Of course he would have been upset," the therapist says. "He experienced loss too."

Sylvie pictures Sandy sitting in a hole with his coat on, smoking a cigarette. He's not alone, though, he's with a girl she's never seen before, she looks Russian, she looks like a model, she's smoking too.

"There wasn't a single thing I wanted to do. Because for years I'd just been an arrow pointing toward Sandy. I hadn't had any interests apart from getting his attention, plus my brain had been pickled by alcohol for years at this point."

Sylvie pictures the backup bottles of vodka she kept under her bed in her twenties. She would start one as soon as she got home from her job at the bookshop. She pictures a cross section of a mug—the largest section vodka, a thin layer of Coke—a diagram in a textbook of how it had to be.

"It doesn't sound like you were in the right place to be in a relationship," the therapist says.

Sylvie stretches out her arms. "It was like I just filled in the gaps of Sandy. Like if you put him in a jar, if he was peach halves, I would be the shape of the syrup in the jar."

"It can be easy to lose yourself when you fall in love," the therapist says.

"The worst thing, though, is that at first it wasn't like that.

We were perfectly balanced, at first. We were sitting balanced, on the scales, and we could look over at each other, look each other in the eye while we were smoking our cigarettes." Sylvie looks over at the therapist, looks at her eyes and tries not to look away.

The therapist's eyes seem to water a little. "That sounds ideal," she says.

"It was. It was really great. And I knew it at the time. I remember thinking: *I'm happy—this is it.* But then the scales tipped."

The therapist nods.

"Something happened in my head when I looked at him. I remember the exact moment—he was wearing a burgundy V-neck and I looked at him and I think I realized just how good-looking he was, and the scales tipped, and he went right up, and I went right down, and I never recovered from that, we never balanced out again."

Sylvie looks across at the therapist's legs and lets her vision blur. "I could have spent the rest of my life just looking at him. He seemed to be golden; I mean, he was, he was golden. I felt like I didn't need anything else. I didn't need to talk or eat or drink. I used to think if I could give him one blow job a day, that was the only sustenance I needed."

Sylvie blushes, hoping the therapist doesn't think she needs to give blow jobs, because if she was with the therapist she would have to do something else, she'd use a different technique.

"We barely ever talked, and if he said anything, he'd often just use one word," Sylvie says.

"One word?"

"Like *yes*, or *very*. Or sometimes, *woof*."

"What does *woof* mean?" the therapist says.

"I don't know," Sylvie says.

"It sounds really nice, the relationship you had together," the therapist says. "It sounds a bit like teenage love. But maybe now you're older you will want to talk more, to get a real connection with somebody."

"I like talking in therapy, but that's because it's the only thing we *can* do."

"Talking in therapy is a good start," the therapist says. "It is structured intimacy, it's one-way intimacy, but it's a safe place for you to learn to think about your feelings and articulate them."

Sylvie takes her cardigan from the back of her chair and puts it around her shoulders. "Me and Sandy did have a real connection. A really strong one. He wrote this thing in my notebook once: *We're like E.T. and Elliott, when you hurt, I hurt.*"

The therapist smiles. "That is really nice."

"I *liked* how he didn't say much. Because he *did* things. He did this thing with our wallets, he put them together and made them kiss. And he used to put little animal statues in my hair when I was sleeping and take photos of them. Everything he did seemed like a poem. He was like a walking poem."

The therapist smiles. "It sounds lovely. I know there were moments of cruelty too. We have talked about how painful that relationship was for you at times."

Sylvie gets a mint from her bag and looks at the therapist. Sandy had stopped letting her come out with him and his friends, because she was too difficult, too shy. She blushed too much, she wouldn't speak, sat at a different table. It had been painful to be left out, but it had been her fault, not his.

"If anyone started talking about their favorite breeds of dog, Sandy would always say, *All dogs are nice.*"

The therapist smiles. "Well, you did leave your room eventually, after you broke up. You didn't turn to pulp on the floor."

Sylvie nods. "I had to go to the launderette to wash my clothes. But, to make myself leave my room . . ."

"What did you do?" the therapist asks.

"I dressed like Sandy. I had a version of his favorite outfit— blue jeans, white T-shirt, navy-blue blazer, white Converse trainers. I wore that and I looked down on my way to the launderette and squinted and it felt like he was with me. I even left my shoelaces untied like he did, and I breathed heavier and took heavier steps."

"Oh, that's sweet," the therapist says.

"I wonder about re-creating that outfit sometimes, still. But I don't think I could."

"You have your own style now," the therapist says.

"Dressing like the past just seems . . . impossible," Sylvie says.

Sylvie looks at the therapist and groans. "I wish we were still together."

The therapist nods softly. "I think just talking about it will help."

"He did say one thing about why our relationship failed, when we got back in touch."

"Oh yes? What did he say?" the therapist says.

"He said *youth*," Sylvie says.

14

IT'S NOT GOING TO HAPPEN

EVEN THOUGH IN THE THERAPY ROOM Sylvie feels she would die from a never-ending orgasm, transforming to a puddle on the floor if the therapist touched her while saying certain phrases—*I can't hug you but I can hold you*—nothing happens when she tries looking at her favorite picture of the therapist, alone in her bedroom. She never gets anywhere near a climax and she doesn't understand why. Is this the one thing a client can never discuss in therapy? If it is, it seems like a glitch. But who could she ask for help in fixing this glitch? *Maybe Conrad*, she thinks.

Sylvie and Conrad had been flatmates in London. They had noticed each other's outward similarities—eating potato chip sandwiches, drinking in their bedrooms, drawing pictures of dogs on walls. And, assuming these things to be indications of inner sameness, they had become friends. They felt that being practically the same person, but one being a boy and one being a girl, they were in a good position to give each other tips on what to do to attract the opposite sex.

You should always wear a cardigan, she used to tell him. *Like Kurt Cobain.*

You should carry small things, sparkling things with jewels, he used to tell her. *Boys like that.*

When Owen had told Sylvie to cut all contact with Conrad, she had stopped texting and emailing him and unfollowed him on social media. She had started calling him on the phone instead, so there would be nothing for Owen to read when he looked through her devices. Conrad was saved as *Clinic* in Sylvie's phone.

Sylvie is lying on the sofa with her feet up, her phone in her hand. "It's frustrating," she says to Conrad, "because in therapy, I'm desperate to roll around on the floor with her for the whole session. It's the number one thing I want to do, the number one thing I think about."

"Roll around doing what?"

"Kissing, stroking hair, holding hands," she says, putting one hand in front of her, staring at it.

"Well, that's not going to happen."

"But if it did, we would know we only have fifty minutes. So to start with, I would take her hand, and look at each finger individually, maybe allowing one minute per finger. We wouldn't talk, there'd be too much to concentrate on."

"Too many fingers," Conrad says.

"Right," Sylvie says, wondering if Conrad likes fingers too. "Because then I'd take her other hand and start on those.

Then we'd put our faces closer together and I'd stroke her hair."

"You know you can't stroke your therapist's hair."

"The light from the window usually comes directly into my face during a session. But we would both be underneath the light, and we'd both be able to see each other equally well."

"Okay," Conrad says.

Sylvie wonders if he's listening on the other end of the line. "It just seems like it would be a quicker way of having therapy work than the *what happened this week, how did that make you feel, have you had that feeling before, when was the first time you remember having that feeling* route. I think it would be a quicker way of making me feel better, happy, and good, if she would roll around on the floor and touch me," she says.

"Well, it sounds like bullshit to me," Conrad says.

"Which version?" Sylvie says. Maybe Conrad isn't the right person to talk to, she thinks. Maybe he's in the camp that disapproves of therapy, but he could never be in that camp if he'd been in the therapy room and felt the therapist looking after him.

"Can't you roll around on the floor with someone else, someone who isn't your therapist?"

"I don't want to do it with anyone else. Who else would I want to do it with? Is there someone available to do it with, that I would like, that I should know about?"

"There probably is, somewhere. I think you need to go on-line. Where do you think you're going to meet someone other-wise; you think you're going to meet someone in Tesco?"

Sylvie makes a noise. "I'm not going online," she says. She wonders if Conrad is looking up a dating site now on a different tab on his phone. Maybe he's looking for somebody for her already. "I can't do online dating," she says. "We would start kissing. I bring mints to therapy anyway."

"It's not going to happen," Conrad says. "Maybe that's why you've decided you want it so much."

"What?" Sylvie says, sitting up with her phone.

"So you can live safely," Conrad says. "If you know it's not going to happen, there's no chance of disappointment, there's no risk of doing something wrong."

"That's not what I'm doing. And wouldn't I be able to get off on her picture if I wanted to live safely?"

"Maybe you've put her too far out of reach for even that to work. You've turned her into a god. Or a pop star. And that means your brain will short-circuit if anything actually happens."

"Maybe." Sylvie gets up off the sofa and goes to look at herself in the lounge mirror. Conrad seems more serious than he used to be. She wonders if he's been maturing since she last saw him. She wonders if all her friends are continuously maturing when she is staying the same.

"She did do this procedure one time, and my brain felt like it was short-circuiting. It was a special procedure with finger movements and eye movements. It had an acronym. ES something. ES . . . X?" she says, still looking at herself in the mirror.

Conrad laughs on the other end of the phone.

"The first thing she did was, she pulled her chair up— nearer to mine. You don't do that in therapy. The chairs always stay put. You don't shuffle them nearer, however you're feeling. You don't change their position."

"Okay," Conrad says.

"Then she told me to picture a calm place."

"I bet you chose your bedroom," Conrad says.

"I did! She asked me to describe the walls in my bedroom. I said they are kind of rhino- or hippo-colored, and there's a dog constellation hanging above my dresser."

"Canis Major?"

"Exactly. When I'd finished describing it, she said, *Nice*. She said the word *Nice*, just by itself."

"Okay," Conrad says.

"Then she started moving her fingers slowly in front of my eyes and told me to follow them with my eyes."

"What was that supposed to do?"

"It was setting a response, a calm response. But . . . I felt excited that she'd moved her chair closer, and excited that she'd said, *Nice*, and *really* excited that her fingers were near my face, and I felt stressed that I wasn't feeling what I was supposed to be feeling. Her fingers were right in front of my face. Very near my mouth!"

Conrad makes a noise down the phone. Sylvie moves over to the bay window and looks out at the street.

"Next I had to think about something stressful. So I thought about what it would be like to bump into Sandy and his wife. And she moved her fingers really fast for this part. But, just, the whole time she was doing it, I was trying not to imagine taking her two fingers for myself, and putting them, putting them . . ."

Conrad snorts. "I thought you liked boys."

"I don't know. Maybe. I think I like the top half of girls and the bottom half of boys? But I mean, hair and eyes and fingers are all, kind of, it doesn't really matter with those parts?"

"Right," he says.

"She has these slender fingers, they look like they're from a fairy tale. And she wears this thick gold ring . . . I just, I feel like, how does she not know, with her long hair, her green eyes, how does she not know that she could be straight from a fairy tale?"

"You're getting pretty excited now," Conrad says, almost shouting. "Can you not do this by yourself? This is what people do, they think all these things, but to themselves, to get themselves off."

"But I need to tell someone to make it more real."

"I have to go," Conrad says. "I have to go tattoo someone."

Sylvie moves away from the window. "What are they having done?" she asks. She wonders if she would feel closer to Conrad if she saw him every day, if she lived on his street. It feels like she's closer to the therapist now than she is to Conrad, it doesn't seem right.

"A dog."

"What breed?"

"It's just . . . a crossbreed, I think. It's their pet, that just died."

"Well, what color is it?" Sylvie says.

"It's brown. I'm using . . ." He pauses and there is a rustling sound. "Chestnut."

"Nice," Sylvie says. "I did ask her for a hug, one time. The therapist."

"And did she give you one?"

"No. She said she couldn't."

"Was that not humiliating?"

"It didn't *feel* humiliating. It felt like everything that happens in the therapy room, it felt like true love."

"Jesus," Conrad says. "I hope you're happy."

"I'm not *happy*," Sylvie says.

When Conrad ends the call, Sylvie sits back on the sofa and opens Instagram. She finds the therapist's personal Instagram account, and holds her phone at the edges, careful not to touch the screen and *like* anything by mistake. She tries to slow down her eyes to take in the grid. Most of the pictures are of the therapist's dog, and Sylvie looks at these first, they don't have the power to hurt her. She feels confident that Butter likes her, he can't ever say anything to make her think otherwise, plus she knows what his life is likely to be like. Sylvie moves on to pictures of the therapist's shadow. She doesn't feel hurt by these either, but nor does she feel excited, she doesn't feel anything for the waste-image of the image she wants to see. The image she wants to see is the therapist with sun on her face. Sylvie decides to let herself watch one video, the video where she can make out the reflection of the therapist's face in the wet sand, if she watches to the end. Butter jumps down from a groyne, he play-bows, a low wave comes, then breaks, then there it is—the face, the hair, the eyes that help her.

Sylvie turns off her phone and looks at herself in the black screen. She thinks, *I'm bleeding off the screen*, and moves her phone back. She thinks, *Jacobean man*, without knowing why. Her forehead looks like a castle wall. She wishes she could see through it and check her brain. She wishes the therapist could, then she'd know what she was dealing with and be in a better position to treat her. Sylvie drives to the seafront. She parks and looks out at the line where the sea meets the sky. She pushes her seat back and stretches out her legs, then picks up one of the parking slips from the corner of the dashboard. After finding a pen on the floor, she starts to draw on the back of it, leaning on her knee. First, she draws the therapist's hair, long straight hair with a middle parting—just the shape of the hair by itself, no face. Then she draws the therapist's sunglasses. The two shapes make Sylvie feel better. She takes a photo of the drawings and sends them to Conrad.

Flash, she writes as a caption.

Conrad messages straight back; he must be on a break. *Of what?* he texts.

The first one is the therapist's hair, the second one, her sunglasses.

The first one, he texts back, *is the outline of a penis, the second, a pair of boobs.*

Sylvie looks at the photos of the drawings and starts to laugh, she grabs the gear stick and wobbles it around. She gets another parking slip and draws a picture of a brain inside a glass dome, sends it to Conrad, then drives up the hill to her house.

15

APPLE CORE

SYLVIE IS WALKING UP THE STAIRS, and the therapist is getting their glasses of water, and Sylvie can hear a vacuum going somewhere in the house. The therapist must have a cleaner and she must have allowed the cleaner to come during Sylvie's slot. The sound of the vacuum is only half-muffled when the therapist shuts the door of the therapy room. There is an apple core on the therapist's side table, starting to brown, and Sylvie waits for the therapist to throw it away but she doesn't, she puts her water down in front of it, which magnifies the apple from where Sylvie is sitting.

The therapist is wearing a lime-green top, for some kind of sports, maybe cycling, made of a shiny modern material with a zip all the way to the chin. Sylvie is wearing what she always wears, her favorite outfit. Sylvie looks at the therapist to try to work out what is going on and notices that the angle of her gaze is wrong. The chairs have been moved, maybe by the cleaner. The therapist isn't smiling and the set of her mouth seems to be unapologetic—for the chairs, the noise, the alien clothing. For the first time since she started therapy, Sylvie doesn't want to be in the room. She wants to leave but she knows she can't. The walls of the room are still there and the time designated for her is going to make sure she takes it. She will have to sit through the fifty minutes. Sylvie knows this is something she can do. It's something she has tools for—she will just run on the lowest level of consciousness. *It's like visiting the care home. It's like sharing a bed.*

Sylvie looks at the therapist and narrows her eyes slightly.

"How have you been?" the therapist says.

"Good," Sylvie says, trying to smile, then looking in the direction of the window and letting her vision blur. "You know I was going to try the book club in the library?"

"Yes," she hears the therapist say. "How was it?"

"It was awful. I really hate talking about books in groups, or talking about anything in groups, really. I left in the break, I ran home."

"And how did you feel at home?"

"Good. Once the feeling of being in a room with strangers that might ask me to speak had worn off."

The therapist smiles and tugs on the sleeves of her top. Sylvie expects the sleeves are uncomfortable, they fall shy of her wrists and look rubbery. She wonders if the therapist will excuse herself to go and change.

"Then, when I was at the beach the other weekend, a woman came up to me and said she'd seen me there, at the book club. She said she'd wanted to leave too but didn't know how. We swapped numbers and talked about what books we like. And we found out we lived in London at the same time, in our twenties. I really like her. We like a lot of the same things."

"That's great!" the therapist says. "I think this is what you need right now—to find your tribe."

"My tribe," Sylvie says, trying to control her smile.

"A real friend," the therapist says.

Sylvie hears the vacuum get closer to the therapy door, then pass.

"I don't know why I didn't tell you about her last session. It was like I was keeping it secret, trying to keep her to myself."

The therapist smiles and nods.

"I kind of can't believe she wants to be friends with me. She has a really good job, she's a curator for performance art, and she has beautiful shiny hair, like a prefect. She's like one of the popular girls at school, but she's nice and into books." Sylvie blushes, feeling it looks like she is trying to punish the therapist for not looking like someone who is into books today with this comment, though that's not what she's trying to do.

"That's great, I'm so pleased you met her," the therapist says, playing with the zip on her top.

"If I was on my way to meet up with her, I'd definitely feel natural and not be wondering what the point of it was," Sylvie says, hoping the therapist realizes she's referencing a discussion from a previous session.

"And have you made plans to meet up?"

"We're going to text. She's called Chloe."

Sylvie gets a mint from her bag. "She looks a bit like this girl I was friends with when I was sixteen. Charlotte. I never understood why Charlotte wanted to be friends with me. I don't think she liked me at all. I think she had an idea of me that was totally wrong, but I tried to play along with it."

"What idea do you think she had of you?"

"I think maybe she thought I was like someone from a different time. Different from all the other kids our age. I remember she wore lace tops sometimes."

"So you thought *she* seemed different, or from a different time?"

"Maybe. She seemed either like someone our age from a long time ago, or like a very old person from our time."

"I suppose that could have been the wrong idea about her too? You might both have had fantasies about each other that weren't quite right, that's not uncommon. But you saw something in each other that you liked, and you enjoyed spending time together?"

"I don't know if we enjoyed spending time together. But we used to write each other letters and leave them under stones for each other. I know we both enjoyed that. The letters felt really important, we connected so well in the letters."

The therapist leans down to tie one of the laces on her trainers; Sylvie waits for her to straighten back up again.

"I suppose I just really wanted to be the kind of person that she liked."

"And what kind of person did you think that was?"

"I imagined her friends being very serious, writing each

other poetry, calling each other in the middle of the night with important things that couldn't wait, giving each other roses. But then I went to Charlotte's bedroom one time, and there was a photo of her with her friends on the wall, and they didn't look like that at all. They were wearing colorful T-shirts, goofing around, laughing. They looked modern."

"And did seeing that they weren't anything out of the ordinary help you relax more with Charlotte?"

Sylvie hears the vacuum approach the therapy door again.

"I don't know. I suppose I never got to find out because we stopped being friends soon after. Because of the chewing gum incident."

"The chewing gum incident," the therapist says.

"It's a stupid story. We were taking a drive, which is the main thing we did together, and I was chewing this gum, but there was something wrong with it—when it mixed with my spit it got bigger and bigger—and it was erupting out of my mouth and I had to ask Charlotte—she was driving—to pull over so I could spit it out."

The therapist nods and frowns.

"I had to spit multiple times to get it all out. And when I'd finished, and straightened myself up in my seat, Charlotte looked over at me with such a look of disgust and said, *That must have been the devil's gum.*"

The therapist widens her eyes slightly.

"And then she drove me home. We didn't speak for the rest of the journey. It was so silent, I remember being scared to swallow. And she didn't call me again after that. That was it."

"Did you call her?" the therapist says.

"No. Because I felt like she'd seen the real me and she didn't like it."

"I'm sure a bad stick of gum doesn't define you," the therapist says. "It seems like that would be a very silly reason for her to not want to be friends."

"I don't think any of her other friends would be forced to spit this disgusting white stuff out at the side of the road," Sylvie says.

The therapist makes a short humming noise. Sylvie wonders if the therapist is more like Charlotte or more like her, and she wonders which she would prefer the therapist to be, and realizes she doesn't know.

"I just hope nothing like that happens with Chloe," Sylvie says.

"I don't think you need to worry about that. Just enjoy having made a new friend."

"I felt so bad for leaving the book club like that without telling anyone. But then that's what made her notice me. I think she liked it."

"Well, leaving somewhere like that shows independence," the therapist says. "And that's attractive."

Sylvie nods. "She told me she hasn't made friends down here because it's so small and she doesn't want to have to bump into people all the time and chat. She wants to be free to sit quietly staring at the sea and not be interrupted."

"But she wants to talk to you," the therapist says.

Sylvie smiles, excited. "She must like what we talk about. I do too. I really don't want to lose her," she says, after a pause.

"You've only just found her," the therapist says, playing with her zip again.

When Sylvie leaves the therapist's house, the sky is overcast and there is a smell of damp dogs on the street as she walks through the static. When she arrives at her front door, for the first time the static doesn't fall away and a fantasy of love doesn't take its place. Sylvie struggles for a minute with the lock and she can hear Curtains starting to alarm-bark through the door. When Sylvie gets in, she rushes straight to the bathroom, puts the toilet lid down, sits on it in her clothes, and unlocks her phone to text Conrad. She rubs Curtains with her foot to calm her.

My obsession with the therapist seems to be over, she texts.

Conrad replies straightaway. *I don't believe you*, he says.

I thought this was what I wanted, but I don't like it at all, Sylvie texts.

Sylvie gives Curtains a pig's ear, then goes up to her bedroom and lies down on top of the covers. She looks at the hippo-colored wall and the Canis Major picture. She says the word *nice* in her head. She looks over at her wardrobe of five white blouses and four black trousers and feels relaxed and says out loud, quietly: "Nice." There is a camel wool coat, unworn, hanging to the side of the trousers. Sylvie had always thought that people wearing camel coats seemed to throb with success, so she had bought one to see if something happened to her character when she wore one. Seeing the coat hanging up makes Sylvie wonder if the therapist's outfit today was somehow a prop. The therapist could have been trying to help Sylvie. She could have been trying to dampen down Sylvie's obsession by wearing the strange top. Maybe she had been provided with the top at supervision after sharing her fear that a client's transference issue was getting out of hand. Maybe this was something that happened. And maybe the therapist had purposefully booked a cleaner to come at the same time as Sylvie's session to try to make Sylvie see she was a regular person who dropped dead skin cells every day and had to participate in the boring task of arranging for them to be cleaned up.

16

THE PENDANT

SYLVIE LOOKS AT HER REFLECTION in the glass of the coffee shop while she waits for Chloe. She remembers Sandy telling her how attractive her reflection was when they were looking in cafés for somewhere to eat. She'd been insulted, but she'd known he was right; she looked a million times better reflected in glass than she did in photographs or mirrors. It's sunny, and Sylvie looks down the street and sees Chloe coming toward her wearing a zipped-up black bomber jacket with a gold necklace falling over the ribbed collar. As Chloe gets nearer, Sylvie sees that the pendant on the necklace is a human figure.

Chloe hands Sylvie a rolled-up magazine. "This has an interview with the author you were reading on the beach," she says.

They go inside and order coffee and Sylvie thinks about how they are separate bodies that have been living in the same town for years, never knowing the other existed, but now they do know the other exists, they are going to sit close to each other, and talk, and compare themselves to see what is different and what is the same.

Sylvie leans forward to look at the pendant on Chloe's necklace. "It's a clown!" she says.

Chloe smiles and bends her head down and puts her chin in the chain and tries to focus her eyes the short distance to the pendant.

"I love clowns," Sylvie says. "Especially the sad ones. I mean, especially Pierrot."

"I love Pierrot!" Chloe says, pronouncing it a different way than how Sylvie pronounces it, pronouncing it Peer-oh.

Sylvie blushes, excited. Nobody ever loves Pierrot, nobody can ever think who he is. "I always wanted a Pierrot bedroom when I was little," she says.

"I had a Pierrot bedroom!" Chloe says. "Well, I had the duvet and pillowcase set."

"What, you actually had one?" Sylvie starts to picture the popular girls at school but tries not to let them come into focus.

Chloe laughs. "Were you not allowed one?"

"I don't know if I was allowed one, I think I instinctively felt that I shouldn't even ask."

"Why?" Chloe says, turning to face Sylvie.

"I felt like I didn't deserve it, maybe?" Sylvie says. "Because I hadn't experienced the things that someone with a Pierrot bedroom should have experienced?"

Chloe fingers her clown pendant. "Oh god. Maybe I didn't deserve it. How do I know if I deserved it?"

"I bet you were one of the girls that deserved it," Sylvie says, smiling.

Chloe looks at her. "I didn't have the lampshade or the curtains, I don't think."

Sylvie laughs.

"I know I didn't have the wastepaper basket," Chloe says. She picks up her phone and opens Instagram to show Sylvie. "Look how many pictures of Pierrot I've posted," she says, scrolling down and stopping to point at Pierrot figures. "I'm always looking out for Pierrot when I go to galleries. I can't believe you like him too."

"I'm always looking out for him in charity shops, in bedding," Sylvie says, and Chloe laughs.

Their coffees are called out and Chloe goes to the counter. Sylvie unrolls the magazine and finds the author interview, but her brain can't slow down enough to read. When Chloe passes her a coffee, Sylvie looks at her ring with the set pearl.

"I've been wondering who you gave the book to," Chloe says. "The one you were reading on the beach. Was it a friend here?"

"I don't really have any friends here," Sylvie says, laughing. "It was . . . my therapist," she says, then she clamps her teeth together and stretches her lips out to the sides.

Chloe widens her eyes. "And did she like it?"

"I don't know. She said she found the style difficult to read, but she didn't say anything about the content, weirdly."

"The content of the shower cubicle," Chloe says, laughing. "The strap-ons in the shower cubicle."

Sylvie snorts.

"I've been trying to find a therapist too," Chloe says. "Is yours any good?"

"She's good," Sylvie says slowly, "but . . . really . . . she's too good?"

"Is there such a thing as too good?" Chloe asks.

"I think so. Things that are too good ruin you for the things that are on a normal level, don't they?"

Chloe looks at Sylvie. "Do they? And what's so good about her?"

Sylvie grimaces. "I spend most of my waking and sleeping hours trying to work that out. But I don't know."

Chloe laughs. A black poodle goes past on a leash and cocks its leg on a chair outside the café.

"I don't know if it's because she's tall and beautiful with super-long hair, or if it's because she lives in a beautiful big house and has a big black car." Sylvie senses that Chloe won't ask her if she's gay, she senses Chloe's brain will have a system of categorization more sophisticated than that.

"So it's not that her sessions are too good? She's not too good at being a therapist? She's just too good at being a person?"

Sylvie makes her hands into fists and leans her chin on them. "I do think she's made a huge success of being a person." She starts to play with her bottom lip. "I feel like she is very big, with this really big life, and I am very small, and everything in my life is small."

"But doesn't that make her a bad therapist if she makes you feel that way?"

"I think she's a good therapist," Sylvie says, frowning, "but I know what you're saying."

"I've been thinking a lot about big and small lives recently," Chloe says. "Like how most of the artists I work with live a small life that leads to a big life. But they don't tend to live medium lives. And I think I'm living a medium life."

"Are you?" Sylvie suddenly thinks the word *medium* is such a beautiful word, perfect for Chloe, and she wants to have a life like that word too. "But isn't a medium life better than a small life?"

"I don't know, I think you can only get to a big life through living a small life, a life without amplification or media or contacts. Because you have to focus, and focus is small."

Sylvie nods. She feels that she should write this down. "But what if your life just stays small, like mine?"

"Well, it's a gamble," Chloe says. "But isn't it, anyway, more satisfying?"

"I wish I had faith that it's the right choice for me. I feel like I'm playing at the vet's. I love the animals, but I feel like the ideal me is somewhere else in a bigger job."

Chloe nods and gets gum out of her jacket pocket and offers a stick to Sylvie. "I wish I dared to choose a small life, but I panic when I feel my life getting small. And I feel happy then going to the gallery, which feels big . . ."

"Your job is brilliant," Sylvie says. "Curating those shows." Sylvie wonders if she could do a medium job at the moment, in the state she's in now, a job where she isn't told what to do all the time, a job that would make her feel older, her age, and more in the world, like Chloe.

"I suppose a lot of what I do at work feels like a trick, though," Chloe says. "Small can feel good and real. And there's less compromise with small. You can be more free."

"The vet's does feel good and real, I suppose. I always want to do what I'm doing, because I want the animals to get better. I never have to lie or feel fake." Sylvie sips her coffee. This is the first time she's seen her job as a choice of where she wants to be as a human, with values of focus and honesty, and she likes how it feels.

When they leave the café, Sylvie holds the rolled-up magazine like a baton. Chloe asks if Sylvie can send her a link to her therapist and Sylvie blushes, nods, puts the end of the rolled-up magazine over her mouth, and starts to breathe through it, in and out.

"I feel like we aren't finished," Sylvie says then, "discussing things."

"We're definitely not finished," Chloe says. "To be continued!"

They each put a hand up and smile, and Sylvie turns around and walks away. She takes the chewing gum out of her mouth and looks for somewhere to throw it, and she notices how much it looks like a brain. She only walks a few steps before getting out her phone, searching for the therapist's website, and sending Chloe a link.

17

THE BOOK KNEW

THE THERAPIST puts their waters on their separate tables and sits down. She is wearing a gray A-line skirt with a powder-blue blouse and a loose blue jumper. Sylvie thinks the therapist looks as good in this outfit as she did in the black trousers and white blouse, maybe even better. She wonders what it means, that the therapist has chosen such a beautiful outfit straight after the outfit last week that seemed designed to put Sylvie off her. The therapist's long peach ponytail lying just above the blue jumper reminds Sylvie of something from a long time ago, or something from a novella, maybe set in Europe.

"How have you been?" the therapist says, smiling and crossing her legs.

Sylvie looks at the line where the therapist's blue jumper meets her gray skirt. "I saw Chloe this week," she says.

"Oh yes?" the therapist says, smiling and leaning forward slightly.

"We *met for coffee*," Sylvie says, wondering if it's still depressing to say that, even when she's using a tone of awareness.

"That's great. Did you have a good time?"

Sylvie smiles and nods. "We have so much in common. We like the same books . . ." Sylvie almost mentions how Chloe likes Pierrot, how she had a Pierrot bedroom, but maybe the therapist will think it a joke, and Sylvie doesn't want to ruin it by talking about it. She pictures Pierrot, standing silently in black-and-white. He wouldn't tell his therapist anything unless he could tell it by mime.

"I'm glad you found each other," the therapist says.

"You know when we were talking about the times I naturally feel like a person? I realize I forgot the main one—when I'm reading."

"Of course! And you feel good when you're reading?"

Sylvie nods. "I think maybe people in books are more what I expect people to be like, rather than the people I meet in real life? Can that be true? That seems stupid."

"Well, you are seeing the inside of a person when you're reading . . . you get to see their thoughts, not just the outside of them. And maybe you find that easier to relate to."

"Right," Sylvie says.

"It reminds me of your idea of videoing yourself so you can see yourself as a person," the therapist says, "but the other way round."

"I'm seeing other people the way I see myself, from the inside," Sylvie says.

"It's probably why a lot of people read—for human connection."

Sylvie plays with her bottom lip.

"But, again, it's one-way intimacy," the therapist says. "The characters in the book don't know you're there. You can't speak to them, you can't join in."

Sylvie gets a mint out of her bag. "One-way like therapy," she says.

"I think you will enjoy two-way intimacy when you're ready," the therapist says.

"I would listen to you talk about yourself during therapy, if I was allowed. We could split the session so it was half-and-half." Sylvie realizes she would hate it if another client talked to the therapist like this, it would be creepy, especially if the client was older, and a man.

The therapist smiles and pulls her skirt over her knees and Sylvie looks away.

"It sounds like you have started building two-way intimacy with Chloe already," she says brightly.

Sylvie nods, but feels worried. "What I don't like about books is the fact that they end. I try not to read right to the end, I like to leave a couple of pages at least, for later."

"For when?" the therapist says. "When is later?"

"Never, I suppose. I just like to know it's there and it's not over." Sylvie thinks about the novels stacked up on her bedside table, the last few pages unread. She gets a mint out of her bag and puts it in her mouth with one that's almost finished.

"I remember Nick used to say he thought books were to blame," she says.

"To blame for what?"

"For making us think we can know another person."

"I think it's possible to get to know another person, over time, if you are honest with each other," the therapist says.

"But it's impossible to know if people are being honest," Sylvie says.

"We are honest in therapy," the therapist says. "This is a good start."

"I'm honest, but you're at work, so it's not the same. You can't really be honest."

"I am at work, you're right. But I'm also being honest. I don't think the therapy would work if I was being dishonest in what I say."

Sylvie looks at the therapist. The idea that she is being honest with Sylvie every week, and honest right now, can't quite make it through a barrier in her brain. Sylvie doesn't think it can be true. She thinks it could only be possible if they held hands, or if their faces were closer together. She imagines her closed mouth near the therapist's cheek, then stops and shakes her head.

"It could have been hard for Nick to connect with other people at that time because of the drugs he was taking. And that would have impacted you. You were probably in very different places."

Sylvie makes a noise. "I just remembered, Nick told me once that the book he was reading knew he was reading it," she says, half-grimacing, half-smiling.

"How so?"

"I don't know. There were always things like that going on with Nick. Things I didn't understand. He showed me this book, this paperback, and it had his surname in the middle of the text, seemingly for no reason. It said *was here* after his surname. Like graffiti. But in the typeface of the book."

"And what was going on there?"

"I found out later it was some kind of phrase from the war that people used to write everywhere, so it must have been referring to that. But when he showed me, I thought it was actually referring to him because he was magic."

"You must have found him fascinating," the therapist says.

Sylvie nods and smiles. "I feel like I would never have got to know Nick, no matter how long I went out with him," she says. "Or Sandy."

The therapist nods and smiles.

"I had this idea once," Sylvie says, "for a game I could play with friends, to see how similar we were on the inside."

"Oh yes?"

"One of us would text a code word, at any time, and the person that received the code word would reply straightaway with what they were thinking at that exact moment."

"That sounds like an interesting exercise. Did you ever do it?"

"I asked Conrad to do it with me."

"And what did he say?"

"He said, *No, thanks,*" Sylvie says, and the therapist smiles.

"You could ask someone else?" the therapist says. "Don't be defeated at the first hurdle."

Sylvie shakes her head. Maybe she wasn't interested in learning what any of her other friends were thinking about, not really.

"I had another idea about how to stop thinking about you so much," Sylvie says, trying to raise the mood in the room.

The therapist smiles and waits.

"I thought I could have therapy too often, if I could work out how to afford it. Like every day, or even a few times a day. The aim would be to have it so much that it would start to get boring, and I'd be like, *Please, no more therapy!*"

The therapist laughs.

"I remember school showed us a video once in PSHE where a father got his son to stop smoking by making him chain-smoke until he threw up. It was horrible, but that's the kind of thing I mean. That's the kind of technique I'm talking about."

18

ELABORATE WAYS

SYLVIE AND CHLOE ARE SITTING on the beach in the same spot where they first met. Between them, Curtains has dug herself a hole in the pebbles to lie in. Chloe and Sylvie are both playing with pebbles, moving them from one hand to the other as they talk, and staring at the sea.

"I hope she has space for me," Chloe is saying.

"Me too," Sylvie says. "Did you mention we were friends? I don't think you should, because of the rules."

"Oh," Chloe says. "I already did. But I don't think it'll matter? It's not like I will be talking about you in therapy. No offense."

Sylvie looks over, and Chloe is pushing her body up on the pebbles so she can adjust her belt, doing the crab with the bottom half of her body.

"I talk about you in therapy sometimes," Sylvie says, "just as an example of a real friend."

"Oh," Chloe says, sitting up again. "That's nice. I'm flattered." She throws the pebble she is playing with toward the sea, but it doesn't quite make it. Then she picks up a new, smaller pebble and passes it from one hand to the other. "Maybe I would talk about you, as an example of someone who is quite free, in a kind of childlike way—a good way. I have to be so grown-up for work now, I feel like I've lost something, I've lost some of that freedom."

"Really!" Sylvie says. She looks over at Chloe, imagines her for a moment in the therapy room, imagines the therapist looking at her. She brings her knees up to her chest then, and lets her head drop to rest on her knees. "But . . . if the therapist hugs you, I won't be able to stand it."

"What?" Chloe says. "I don't want a hug, I'm not going there for a hug."

Sylvie opens her mouth and scrapes the tops of her knees with her front teeth.

"Oh god," Chloe says softly. "Do you have that thing? What is it called? The thing that happens. I mean love, but also . . ."

"Transference?" Sylvie says into her knees.

"That's it!" Chloe leans over to put a hand on Sylvie's shoulder. She falls onto Curtains as she leans and Curtains yelps.

"Sorry! Remind me of your dog's name?"

"It's Curtains," Sylvie says.

Chloe nods solemnly. "What are you going to do about the therapist?"

"Nothing! What can I do? I'm just going to do nothing and then I'm going to die."

Chloe smiles. "But have you told her?"

"I told her ages ago. You tell them everything in therapy."

"You do? Wasn't it hard to say that?"

"There were a couple of false starts when it seemed like it wouldn't physically come out of my mouth. But when I eventually said it, it was just like nothing, like water."

"And what did she say?"

"She said it was normal."

"Normal!" Chloe says, and starts to play with her pebble again. "Normal," she repeats, more slowly.

"It seems too intense to me to be normal. It's like a crazy drug but without the comedown afterward, without the hangover. If I'm having a bad day, say if I'm feeling lonely, or empty, I just turn away from whatever I'm doing, mentally, and think about her, and I immediately feel ecstatically happy."

"Wow," Chloe says.

"Also, if I see her between sessions, by chance—in the supermarket, or at the petrol station—it makes me *shake* with happiness for hours afterward."

"God! It's like she's a pop star to you. Have you seen *Der Fan*? About a schoolgirl who's obsessed with this lead singer?"

Sylvie shakes her head. "It sounds good. Should I watch it? Is it a happy ending? Do they find happiness forever?"

"I mean, not really," Chloe says.

"I keep thinking of elaborate ways to get the therapist to hug me. I start thinking, *Maybe if I left the country, changed my name, then stayed in that country for six months, then came back,*

changed my address, changed my hair color, maybe she would be
allowed to hug me then."

"But you'd still be her client. Her ex-client?"

"If I changed my sex. If I changed everything and didn't sign on as her client when I was the second version of me."

Chloe makes a noise.

"I don't think I've ever wanted anything so desperately. It reminds me of when I was little, and we went to pick up our puppy—we'd chosen one and I'd named her Mickey—but when the breeders asked my dad what he thought about dogs, he said he didn't like them. So the breeders got up, took Mickey back, and just left us sitting in their garden. We never got the puppy. It feels like that, but way worse."

Chloe shakes her head. "Are you sure you don't mind if I start seeing her too?" she says.

"I can come pick you up after a session, maybe," Sylvie says. "And we can discuss how it went."

Chloe tilts her head.

"I do want you to get the benefit and happiness of seeing her, because you're my friend."

"Okay," Chloe says.

"If she likes you more than me, I can handle it," Sylvie says, "because I like you more than me."

"Sylvie," Chloe says. "Don't say that. And she's not going to like me more, that's not going to happen."

Sylvie half shrugs. "I'm also interested to see if she puts a spell on you too," she says.

Chloe laughs. "I really don't think that will happen."

"But we're so similar."

Chloe smiles. "I know. But I don't think I have the ability

to be swept away like that. Not anymore. I kind of wish I did. I loved that ability. The special skill of the teenager."

Sylvie snorts, then lies down, shuffling her body into the pebbles. She puts one arm over her eyes to shield them from the sun. "You don't know what will happen when she smiles at you, though. I think it's her smile that does it. It's her smile that sets it off, the magic."

Chloe smiles and lowers herself sideways onto the pebbles and props her head up with one hand to look at Sylvie. Between them, Curtains gets up and circles in the pebbles three times before lying back down in the same spot.

"I can't believe *you*—a real friend—will be in the same room as the therapist, my one form," Sylvie says, smiling.

Chloe laughs and twists her body to get gum out of her pocket. "Your one form?"

Sylvie nods.

"I guess that's the problem, with a crush," Chloe says, "with love. There's only one object. It's not like a can of Coke; there aren't many versions of her, readily available, all over the world."

"But in my imagination she's readily available," Sylvie says. "Also I can google her wherever. Almost like a can of Coke."

"But is that enough—seeing a picture of her on a screen or in your mind?"

Sylvie lifts her arm away from her eyes and shifts to her side to face Chloe. "If I can keep up the fantasy or the hope that one day it will be more than that, then it's enough."

"But how long can you keep that up?"

Sylvie shrugs and strokes Curtains's head. She doesn't

think there will be a time when she will have to evaluate reality, separate her fantasy from it, and discount it completely. When will that time be? People seem to think there's a time that you're aiming for that will be representative of your life, your *real life*, but Sylvie doesn't think that. Maybe the day before she dies, maybe on her deathbed, maybe that will be the time she'll see what was fantasy and what was not. And the therapist will already be dead at that point, she hopes.

"I know it's actually super-hard to crush hope," Chloe says. "Hope can basically live off any tiny little scrap."

Sylvie nods. "I'm aware I'm allowing myself to exist in a pathetic situation," she says quietly.

Chloe shakes her head. "I think it was brave to tell her how you feel."

Sylvie makes a noise. "Wouldn't it have been braver to have kept it to myself? If there's no risk in therapy, can there be any bravery? I feel like I've just transferred the burden of my obsession onto her."

"I doubt it's much of a burden. She's probably flattered—look at you."

"I can't," Sylvie says, and when they both laugh, Sylvie feels there's nothing better than being immediately understood by Chloe.

"I used to always be caught in some terrible obsession or other. I know it can feel so painful, but I still miss it," Chloe says. "I miss the intensity, how all-consuming it feels, how the obsession becomes the meaning of your life."

"In your teens?" Sylvie says.

"Well, yes . . . but in my twenties too."

Sylvie smiles at this.

"The best one was Tom," Chloe says. "He was a pianist, he lived in Highgate, and he had brown hair in curtains."

"God," Sylvie says.

"And I never knew where I stood with him, which made it a perfect breeding ground for obsession. I used to send him long letters, and he'd say things like: *Let's just see what happens.* It drove me insane."

"You're just like me!" Sylvie says. "In fact, I was telling my friend Conrad about you the other day. My old flatmate in London. I told him, *I know you'll like her, she's like me, but the successful art version of me.*"

Chloe laughs.

"And Conrad said: *You're the successful art version of you.*"

"He's right!" Chloe says, and Sylvie smiles and shakes her head and reaches over to play with Curtains's ear. Talking to Chloe has never made Sylvie feel bad, not even for a second. She wonders if it will always be like this.

"I can't believe I told the therapist I think about her six hundred times a day."

Chloe laughs. "Little does she know it's six hundred and one."

Sylvie snorts. "I know I'm putting myself way down on the scales, on the seesaw, by putting her so high up."

"I mean, she's the perfect obsession. She *has* to stay distant, she has to be up there. You can never be equal. That's the contract. She can never really hug you, never really be your friend."

Sylvie and Chloe both sit up. Their hair blows over their faces in the wind. Sylvie thinks of the words *never really* and wonders where they sit on the fantasy–reality spectrum.

"But it makes perfect sense that you would fall in love with her," Chloe says. "It makes sense you'd fall for somebody out of reach, who can't hurt you, after being with Owen, who was so controlling."

Chloe gets up and stands in front of Sylvie, holding her hands out in an offer to pull her up. She is standing between Sylvie and the sun, and the sun is low, and it creates a golden halo all around her from where Sylvie is sitting.

"What happened with Tom?" Sylvie asks.

Chloe shakes her head. "He went on tour in Europe. He sent me a postcard from Germany with a quote from Karl Valentin, this kind of German version of Charlie Chaplin. *The future used to be better*, that was the quote. I felt like he was telling me to stop. Stop writing to him, stop wanting him, he had other things in mind. I cried for a few weeks, then signed up for piano lessons."

"Wow. Can you still play?" Sylvie says.

"A little. I can play 'Ode to Joy,'" Chloe says. "Shall we go get a Coke from Hades?" she says then. "It's actually open today."

Sylvie smiles and reaches out her hands to get pulled up, then she picks up Curtains and they set off down the underground promenade, on their way to Hades.

19

GHOST MOTHER

AT WORK, there is a column in the appointments diary that is colored red. It's for emergencies only. Sylvie scans the column, she checks that the therapist's surname isn't there, then she checks that the breed of the therapist's dog isn't there. Some emergencies don't call first, they just arrive, there isn't time to call if the animal needs oxygen or if it is bleeding to death, so Sylvie goes to reception and scans the parking lot. She checks that there are no cars the same make and color as the therapist's car or the therapist's husband's car, and she checks the number plates.

While she stands at reception, she imagines it happening— she imagines the therapist's car approaching, the therapist rushing in with Butter in her arms, and Butter gasping or bleeding from a dog fight or being hit by a car. Sylvie hears her pulse in her head. Would she hug the therapist? First she would take the dog from her, carefully, and she would rush him to prep. She would turn on the oxygen quicker than any other person in the world would be able to turn on the oxygen. She would shout for a mask, she would shout for a vet. And after that, when Butter was stable, would she hug the therapist? Maybe she would just put a hand on her back, rub it a little. She could lean in for a full hug then, if the therapist seemed to need it, if she was crumbling.

The second nurse comes in through reception to start her shift, and Sylvie smiles at her and wonders if she's disappointed to see she'll be working with Sylvie. The nurse's dog comes in behind her, off-leash, and Sylvie puts a hand out to say hello, but the dog runs past.

"He's not interested," Sylvie says, and makes a sad face at the receptionist. The receptionist smiles, then rolls her chair over to the printer.

"She," the other nurse says as she walks past. "She's a she."

"Right," Sylvie says. "Sorry." Sylvie goes through to the ward and sprays down the surfaces and rubs them dry and after a while she stops smiling.

There are no inpatients, and Sylvie cleans the lint from the dryer, then takes the towels out and starts to fold them slowly, arranging them by size. She feels heavy with boredom, conscious of doing a lowly job. Feeling low on the list of humans, she imagines herself in the ancient past and it feels okay like that, and then she imagines herself as an old lady and it feels okay like that too, for a moment. But she feels like she needs to do something to curb the feeling that she's getting closer to dying, so she gets her phone out of her tunic pocket and opens the therapist's Instagram page. She puts her phone down by the side of the towels and scans it as she folds and sees there is a new picture. It isn't of the therapist, it isn't of a person, it's just objects. Sylvie holds a towel to her stomach and bends forward and taps on the post to enlarge it. It's a kitchen table with presents and cards arranged around a vase of pink roses. Sylvie zooms in to see if she can read the name written on the cards, and she makes out the therapist's name on all of them. The post must be for the therapist's birthday, and if Sylvie checks the date on the post she will know the date of the therapist's birthday and then she'll know it next year too, and every year after that. Sylvie sees that the post went up forty-seven minutes ago, today. She clicks on her phone to see what date it is. It's the thirteenth of October. *What?* she thinks. *Oh my god.*

She texts Chloe, *Are you there*, and Chloe replies straight-away that she is.

It's the 13th of October, Sylvie texts, *my mum's birthday.*

Chloe sends a broken heart emoji and a birthday cake emoji and *XXX*.

And Chloe, I just went on Instagram and looked at the therapist's page, and it's her birthday too. Today.

What! Chloe says.

I know, Sylvie says.

Oh my god! Chloe says, with a heart emoji.

Sylvie sends an emoji of a brain exploding. She feels like screaming and running up and down the ward.

This is big. What does it make the therapist?

My ghost mother? Now I want to text them both happy birthday but I can't text either of them happy birthday. One because of the boundary of death, and one because of the boundary of the therapist–client relationship.

The ward door opens and a vet's face appears and Sylvie quickly puts her phone into her tunic pocket.

"I've just done a guinea pig PTS," the vet says. "Could you bag it for me? It's in prep."

Sylvie nods and smiles and when the vet leaves, she texts Chloe, *to be continued*, then picks up a small bag and a cable tie from the high shelf and takes them to prep. She takes a stethoscope from its hook and puts it to the guinea pig's chest, she closes her eyes and listens, holding her breath, until she's sure she can hear nothing, not the faintest tap, then she picks up the body and lowers it into the bag. She pulls the cable tie shut and starts on the paperwork, filling in the date slowly.

"It would have been my mum's birthday today," she whispers to the bag. "And it's my therapist's birthday." She puts the paperwork in a tray, saying, *The one form*, in her head, then carries the bag with its warm weight against her stomach down the stairs, keeping her mouth closed. She wonders if the magic of the shared birthday is what has been making the therapist feel so important to her all this time. When she gets to the basement, Sylvie remembers the book she'd had as a child in which a loaf of bread started talking. The bread said, *Mama, Mama*, and people were afraid of it until a worm decided to eat a tunnel through it to discover a talking doll at its center. The doll had been dropped in the batter and baked inside the bread. Sylvie holds her breath and opens the freezer lid and drops in the bag, then lets the lid fall shut. She turns away and breathes again and says, "*Mama . . . Mama . . .* ," and sets off back up the stairs.

20

THE LONG WAY

THE THERAPIST COMES INTO THE ROOM wearing a cream dress. She tucks the skirt between her legs when she sits down and crosses her legs to keep it there. Sylvie looks around the room for birthday cards, for any sign of a recent birthday, but she can't see any—nothing looks different in the therapy room. The therapist smiles and asks Sylvie if there's anything in particular she would like to talk about.

"It was my mum's birthday last week," Sylvie says quickly. "I mean, it would have been. On the thirteenth," she says, and she starts to blush.

The therapist nods and looks at Sylvie and Sylvie looks away.

"That must have been a difficult day for you," the therapist says. "Did you do anything special?"

"I was at work. I'd actually forgotten about it, until I had to fill in the date on a form for a euthanasia." Sylvie feels sick for a quick second, imagining she might have *liked* something on the therapist's Instagram page by mistake, shown she'd been looking.

The therapist frowns and nods.

"I messaged Chloe about it, and she brought me round a box of doughnuts when I got home from work."

"That's so nice. I'm glad you've found a friend that looks after you like that."

Sylvie sees now that the therapist isn't going to acknowledge that it had been her birthday too. And she thinks she can tell, by the way the light bounces off her hair and around the room, that the therapist knows that Sylvie knows that she has the same birthday as Sylvie's mother. She wonders if the therapist finds the coincidence meaningful, if it makes her want to take extra-special care of Sylvie. But then she wonders if the therapist thinks Sylvie might have found out the date of her birthday first, then fabricated the story that it was her mother's birthday on that same date. It seems like a classic thing that a person with attachment problems would do. Sylvie finds that her mouth is all of a sudden filled with saliva and she coughs, choking on it noisily.

"Sorry," she says, blushing, and the therapist smiles.

"Sometimes I feel like you're making me addicted to you by smiling at me," Sylvie says, when she has recovered.

The therapist raises her eyebrows. "I don't want you to be addicted to me, or to anything. Would you prefer it if I didn't smile at you? I don't know if I'd be able to keep that up. I think it would feel a little unfriendly."

"No, no, it would be awful. I just, I sometimes worry that I'm still feeling like this about you." She leans down to get a mint out of her bag.

The therapist frowns. "Is it changing at all?"

"I guess I used to think about you about six hundred times a day and now it's maybe four hundred."

"So it's getting better," the therapist says, smiling.

"I just want to be next to you every second of my life. I feel like that's the only thing I really want."

The therapist nods. "You know, that sounds almost like religion. It sounds almost like how somebody in a cult would talk about their cult leader."

Sylvie feels slightly sick. "That's funny. I told my dad once that I wished Charles Manson was still around so I could be one of his followers."

"But don't you think you would be letting yourself down, blindly following somebody like that?"

"Well, I grew out of wanting to be in the Manson family. But you're helping me, everything you're doing is good. And I just feel so grateful."

"You feel grateful," the therapist says, seeming to vibrate a little, seeming surprised. "That's really nice. But you know, you don't need to be grateful, because this is my job. And you're doing the work too. We are doing the work together."

Sylvie stretches her legs out in front of her, then balls her hands into fists and stretches her arms out.

"We are getting you back from a situation where nearly everything you did was controlled by your boyfriend, by Owen," the therapist says. "I think you needed to put your trust in me, as your therapist, to be able to do that work together. But I don't want you to lose yourself in the process. The work is about finding yourself again."

Sylvie nods. "I know. I just, I feel kind of helpless when I think about you." As soon as she says this, Sylvie feels an attraction for the therapist so pure it feels like its own element, like gold.

"I think it's okay for now," the therapist says. "Like all relationships, it will change, over time."

Sylvie wonders if other people think this, if it is a generally accepted phenomenon that relationships change over time. She'd never considered it to be something that happens.

"Sometimes I try to put myself off you," Sylvie says, "by imagining you watching reality TV in a dressing gown all evening. Maybe you do that. I don't know."

"Maybe I do," the therapist says, laughing.

"Or I picture you eating foie gras, wearing a fur coat, belowdecks on a yacht. But it doesn't do anything, it doesn't work."

"Maybe you don't really believe those images."

Sylvie nods and clasps her hands together. "I thought of another tactic recently that I thought might be more likely to work." Sylvie wonders if she is going to say it, then she knows she's going to say it and wonders why she doesn't stop herself, wonders why she doesn't worry that saying it will put the therapist off her.

"It's not that I want this to happen," Sylvie says. "I just had an idea, and I thought—*that might actually work.*"

"Okay," the therapist says.

The therapist's tone sounds hesitant. Sylvie thought she would be eager to hear her idea, something unusual and most likely intense. The phrase *the work* goes through Sylvie's mind, and she wonders if the work is this: having to decide what to reveal and what to keep hidden. It's hard, it does feel like work, and she doesn't want to do it, she wants to just reveal everything.

"I thought it would help if your husband . . ." Sylvie says, and then she stops.

The therapist's face drops a little but she recovers quickly and nods, and Sylvie thinks the less awkward route now would be to finish her sentence.

"If your husband . . . beat me up, because of how much I like you." When Sylvie has finished speaking she looks to the corner of the room.

"That's awful," the therapist says, her tone sounding strained.

Sylvie keeps her face directed at the corner of the room and doesn't move. She waits for the moment to pass. She thinks of the word *ugly*.

"It's not going to happen," the therapist says, her voice sounding softer now.

"I know," Sylvie says quietly. "I'm sorry."

"You don't have to be sorry. It was just a thought. We've talked about how thoughts aren't always things you believe or things you want to happen. Thoughts aren't facts. We have so many thoughts per day! And they don't stay in our heads for very long at all. This was just one thought that you had."

"I think I just wanted a shortcut."

"A shortcut to . . ." the therapist says.

"To stopping feeling?" Sylvie says.

The therapist nods. "Well, you are familiar with violence

cutting off feeling. That was your experience growing
were hit when you showed emotion. You said your fatı
peared as Hitler in the 'opening credits' of your nightma.
I won't forget that."

Sylvie nods, feeling guilty, as if she had fabricated th.
detail, although she hadn't.

"So it's not at all surprising that violence would present
itself as a solution to you. But we're not going to do that. We
can go the long way in therapy, we don't need to take a
shortcut."

"What will the long way be like?"

"Like this. Talking about your feelings, trying to understand them together, thinking of alternatives that might feel
healthier."

Sylvie can barely believe that the therapist is going to
carry on the session with her. It almost sickens her, that what
she said wasn't enough to make the therapist call it a day, to
make her pass Sylvie on to somebody else.

"It's important to feel your feelings, not to cut them off,
and certainly not to cut them off with violence."

"Okay," Sylvie says, vibrating a little, but not sure if she's
feeling comfort or irritation. Then she says, "I just remembered
this thing that happened with a boy I liked in London."

The therapist nods.

"He worked in Shoreditch in a record shop. I used to go
and stare at him on my lunch break to cheer myself up."

The therapist smiles. "Did you buy a lot of records?"

"No, that's the thing, I feel like I was such a fake." Sylvie
rubs her knees. "I used to go in and flick through records,"
she says, acting out flicking through records with her fingers,

"and I'd look up at this boy, then I'd look down and flick through records again, totally unable to see what records I was flicking through because I was so excited, my eyes couldn't focus properly."

"I don't see what's fake about that. I think it's a nice image of youth. It's normal to want to look at people you like when you're young."

Sylvie frowns. "I wish I'd gone in looking for a specific record and started talking to him naturally, about the record."

"How did you start talking to him?"

"I didn't talk to him in the record shop. I couldn't have talked to him when I was sober, during the day. He was just so beautiful."

The therapist smiles. "I think this is just where you get your kicks from."

"From staring at people I like and not talking to them?"

"Yes. I can see that you get a lot of enjoyment from it. Maybe this is just your thing."

Sylvie laughs. She can't stop herself from smiling. She feels something rising and expanding in her chest, she supposes it's pride, that this might be her thing, that she might have a recognizable thing, and the therapist has recognized it.

"And what happened with this boy?" the therapist says.

"He moved away to Berlin. Then I got hold of his email address somehow and sent him a story I'd written about him. A fantasy, about what happened in the basement of the record shop."

"That sounds nice," the therapist says.

"He said the story was *below par*. But at least he wrote back."

"I suppose that was honest of him."

Sylvie nods. "We emailed a few times. Then one evening I got a text from him. It said: *I'm not here often. Peace.*"

Sylvie looks at the therapist. "I was very excited."

The therapist laughs.

"I texted back, and we arranged to meet up that night. I got really drunk before I left the house and got a taxi to meet him at On the Rocks. He'd shaved his head, he'd shaved his long hair off, so I wasn't even sure if it was him."

The therapist nods.

"But it was. We talked about his hair later. I said I thought it was a real achievement to grow your hair as long as you possibly could, and he said he thought the opposite—that short hair was more honest, that you should aim to take up as little space as possible."

The therapist waits.

"The date was good, from what I can remember. He texted me the day after with just the word *Magic*. That's the nicest response to a date I've ever had. But then he went back to Berlin, and I didn't hear from him, and I was just obsessed with him."

The therapist gives Sylvie a look.

"I know. All I could think was: *When will I visit? Will he move back over? How will we do this?*"

"You felt you were a couple already, because the date went well," the therapist says.

Sylvie nods. "And because I felt this thing I hardly ever

feel. Happiness, I think? And I was desperate to hold on to it."

"People can take time to know if they want to be with somebody," the therapist says. "You don't meet somebody and immediately know you want to spend the rest of your life with them."

"*I* do," Sylvie says.

The therapist smiles.

"And Chloe does. She said the first time we spoke she knew we were going to be friends forever."

"That's really nice," the therapist says. "But I think it's unusual."

"Well, I messed it up with this boy, in the usual way. I told him I wanted to beat him up. I actually emailed him: *I really want to beat you up.*"

"Because you hadn't heard from him?"

Sylvie nods. "And then he called me on the phone from Germany. He said I couldn't say things like that to him. And he was right."

"He didn't know you well enough to know that you didn't really mean it."

Sylvie nods. "He didn't want anything to do with me after that." Sylvie realizes she would never feel like beating the therapist up, she would never say something like that to the therapist, however much she might let her down, or ignore her, in the future.

"I think this has just been the way you talk when you are trying to protect yourself from pain," the therapist says. "But we can find another way of communicating that will make more sense to other people, and that will feel more real to you."

Sylvie nods and smiles.

There are scratching noises at the door, and the door starts to open slowly, as if by itself, and the therapist's dog comes in. Sylvie leans down and stretches out her hand.

"Did he ever bite you again?" Sylvie says.

"No." The therapist lifts her hand to look at the scar. "I think that was a one-off. It was just a bad situation, he was redirecting when he was angry at another dog. I don't think he even realized it was my hand he was biting."

Sylvie smiles. "Butter," she says, and she rubs her fingers together. "Come here." Butter doesn't come to her, and Sylvie leans down to get a mint out of her bag. When she leans back in her chair, Butter jumps up onto her lap.

"He likes you," the therapist says, smiling, and Sylvie considers asking if he sits on any other clients' laps, but she doesn't want to know, so she doesn't ask, she just strokes his white fur, and it sheds off quickly onto her lap, onto her black trousers.

21

VIOLENT SILENCE

SYLVIE IS SITTING ON A BENCH outside Hansen's. She has ordered two coffees for herself and one for Chloe. She feels on edge, too agitated to be out. She considers leaving quickly and texting Chloe an apology, but then she sees Chloe approaching and as soon as Sylvie looks at her face, she feels fine, good, and happy to be out.

"I still can't believe the revelation about the therapist's birthday," Chloe says as she sits down.

Sylvie smiles and takes a sip of coffee and her eyes are bright.

"It must mean something," Chloe says.

"I know. I wish the therapist had said something, I wish she could have admitted it was her birthday too."

Chloe nods quickly and sips the coffee that Sylvie passes her.

"We used to buy my mum a box of Black Magic chocolates for her birthday every year, and I really wanted to buy a box for the therapist, when I found out."

Chloe smiles. "Maybe next year? You could do it anonymously, run up and put it outside her front door the night before. Or I could. We could do it together! As a new ritual."

"That sounds so fun. I'd love to do that. Dressed all in black like the Black Magic man."

Chloe laughs.

Sylvie pictures her and Chloe jumping around in the dark outside the therapist's big house, wearing long black coats, looking more like the girl who microwaved her mum's pearls in *Pump Up the Volume* than the Black Magic man.

"We couldn't leave them on the ground, though," Sylvie says, "or anywhere her dog could get to them. It could kill him, that much dark chocolate."

"Could it really?" Chloe says.

Sylvie nods, feeling concerned. She pictures herself checking dark chocolate on the toxicity wheel at work, seeing the word *EMERGENCY* in red, then she looks down at her coffee and her face crumples. "I said something so bad in therapy last week," she says.

Chloe looks at Sylvie and waits, moving her hand slowly over the table toward Sylvie's.

"I told the therapist I wanted her husband to beat me up, to try to stop my obsession."

"Whoa," Chloe says, putting her hand over Sylvie's. "You're so brave, to actually say that."

Sylvie grimaces. She doesn't think Chloe will be able to make her feel okay about this.

"It's good. I think it's great, actually, that you can be so honest. Almost like a . . . child."

"Or like a freak," Sylvie says. "I feel like I should be tagged or something." She stretches one leg out under the bench, then starts drinking her second coffee. "I feel like she needs to get a restraining order. This is how I felt with Sandy when he stopped liking me. I mean, I felt like beating myself up."

Chloe smiles sadly.

"Sometimes I think I loved Sandy so much that I messed it up on purpose. I think I knew I was doing it—destroying the lovely thing we had. And now I'll never meet anyone else I'll love like that, ever again."

"You sound like someone with a Pierrot bedroom," Chloe says.

Sylvie starts laughing. "Oh god," she says, "that's exactly who I am."

Chloe smiles.

"I've finally made it," Sylvie says.

Chloe laughs.

"I still dream about Sandy so regularly, and we split up years ago! And I still have dreams with Nick in them too. I dream about a boy who's ignored me for years, and a boy who's been dead for years . . ."

"Well, I think it makes you a good person. Maybe it's part of why I like you. It's so obvious that you're made up of longing."

"But wouldn't I be a better person if I'd been able to get the person I loved?"

"But if you had him, it would have turned into something else. Fear of losing him, or complacency, or boredom . . ."

"Not boredom," Sylvie says. "Not with Sandy . . ."

"But you wouldn't feel the longing anymore," Chloe says. "I just think . . . it's a beautiful thing. Like the teenage years when we started to write poetry. Like my Tom years, all those letters I wrote him. The place of longing is the same place as the place of creativity: I read that recently."

Sylvie smiles. She wonders what their friendship would be like if she had a partner and was happy with them. Would she and Chloe still know how to talk to each other, to make the world make sense?

"There was this one time Sandy kissed me when I was asleep," Sylvie says. "And I don't know what happened, but when I woke up it was like another dimension. It was like we were in a different world." Sylvie can remember just the boundaries of that feeling, and she realizes she never got drunk enough to get close to the magic of it again, though she tried every day for years.

Chloe nods and smiles.

"We used to get ready to go out listening to the *Willy Wonka* soundtrack," Sylvie says. "Sandy really liked *Willy Wonka*. Especially the way he pretends to be an old man and he comes out hobbling with a stick when he meets the golden ticket winners, then all of a sudden launches into a forward roll."

"Oh god," Chloe says. "These boys from our pasts, I feel like they could kill us."

"Could you play me 'Ode to Joy' one time?" Sylvie asks.

Chloe nods and smiles. "I'm sorry that it didn't work out for you, with Sandy," she says.

"I threw a book at him once, near the end," Sylvie says, frowning. "He'd gone to a party without me. He told me he didn't invite me because he knew there were going to be famous people there, and he thought I'd act too shy."

Chloe shakes her head.

"I didn't think my shyness was that bad; I thought it was okay, maybe interesting, even. But it wasn't, it wasn't acceptable."

Sylvie feels a sick horror that she can't go back in time and just drop the book on the floor.

"I think I really scared him that night I threw the book," she says.

Chloe frowns and squeezes Sylvie's hand. "What book was it?"

"It was only a paperback, and very slim. It wasn't at all heavy."

"But what was it about?" Chloe says.

"It was black, it was a rare one," Sylvie says. "A compilation of different writers. *Violent Silence*. I think that was the title."

Chloe nods.

"I have it under my bed. I could lend it to you if you like."

"Yes, please," Chloe says.

They both finish their drinks and stand up at the same time.

"I know it was bad," Sylvie says. "Throwing the book. I'd never do anything like that now. Not in real life."

22

HARLEQUIN

SYLVIE SETS OFF FOR HER SESSION a few minutes earlier than usual and waits at the therapist's front door, trying to slow down her breathing. She watches two girls play on a see-saw in the playground on the other side of the road. When the therapist opens the door, her hair is slightly damp, as if she hadn't given herself enough time to get ready, to dry it. Sylvie wonders if the therapist is uncomfortable with wet hair. She wonders if she should offer to wait, if the therapist wanted to go and finish drying it. Maybe she could even offer to dry it *for* her. They could start the session like that, talking to each other through the mirror, optimistic. But something stops Sylvie from offering any of this, and she goes up the stairs as normal, singing, *One, two, three, shake your body down.*

The therapist is wearing a blue shirtdress with a brown

belt, tan tights, and brown sandals. She smiles and asks Sylvie if she has had a good week, and Sylvie tells her that she had felt bad all week for mentioning the thoughts she had been having about the therapist's husband.

"I shouldn't talk about your husband," Sylvie says.

"You don't have to censor yourself in therapy. You can talk about whatever's on your mind. In fact, it's essential to do so."

"But there must be some things that are off-limits?"

"No!" the therapist says brightly.

"I really felt like you wouldn't be here today," Sylvie says after a pause. "I felt like I'd messed this up. I was so happy when you answered the door."

"You thought I wouldn't be here? But of course, of course I would be here."

Sylvie makes her hands into balls and smiles. She is happy to get away from last week, she's glad new days always push old days into the past. She's in the good books again. She keeps the sound of the therapist's *of course* safe in her mind so she can bring it out when she's alone after the session.

"Do you ever worry that you'll wake up one morning and look out your window and all your clients will be there lined up, desperate to see you?"

"No, I don't ever worry about that," the therapist says, smiling.

Sylvie looks down at her feet and imagines herself in the line, with three tall men with curly hair in line ahead of her.

"Imagine if they were all standing in line crying, or trying to throw roses up to the therapy room, or something," Sylvie says.

"I don't think that's going to happen," the therapist says, still smiling.

Sylvie likes imagining queuing outside, but there's no way she would actually do something like that, especially when she thought she'd crossed the line last week into the realm of the unacceptable. But she hadn't. She is still allowed to be here, she is still allowed to talk to the therapist.

The therapist says sorry, that she has forgotten their glasses of water, and goes downstairs, and when she is alone in the room Sylvie lets out a long breath and takes her cardigan off and puts it around the back of her chair. She scans the therapist's bookshelf as she does this, trying to find a book she has read, but all she sees are textbooks. She sits back down and looks toward the window and she thinks about the Pierrot picture book she'd had as a child. There were no words because Pierrot never spoke. It was a story just in pictures—Pierrot throwing a rose up to the window of the girl he loves, then a sneering man reaching across the girl to catch the rose himself. Harlequin. Sylvie looks at the open therapy door and wonders if there would be someone waiting behind the therapist, ready to catch the rose if Sylvie managed to throw one up. The therapist's husband would! He would be there, of course. Sylvie gets her cardigan from the back of her chair and puts it back on, and wonders whether the rose's thorns will hurt the therapist's husband's hand, maybe lead to sepsis. She pictures him drawing a line on his hand to mark where the redness ends, so he can check if it is spreading. Then the therapist comes in with their glasses of water and puts them on their separate tables.

"Do you mind if Butter comes in?" the therapist says. "He's been following me."

Sylvie says she would like him to come in, and Butter comes in and jumps straight onto the window ledge, then lies down and looks out the window.

"Do you know what I just thought?" Sylvie says.

"What did you just think?"

"I just thought: I wonder if he's looking for *me* out there."

The therapist laughs. "But you're in here," she says.

"I know! I just had that thought, for a split second. I do feel that it seems more likely that I would be outside than inside."

"Why is that?"

"I don't know . . . I feel like I shouldn't be allowed entry, maybe. Like your house is in the world for successful people."

The therapist smiles. "Well, there is only one world. There isn't a successful world and an unsuccessful world."

"It feels like there is, and you are in a different world from me."

"We are both in the same world," the therapist says. "We both walk our dogs on the same hill. There is only one world. People can't be split into successful people and unsuccessful people. People are just people."

Sylvie looks up. She wonders if the therapist believes this, and if she would still believe it if she had a low-paid job, lived in a tiny house, drove a cheap car, had no partner.

"We all need the same things," the therapist says. "We all need food, shelter, companionship. Some people have more money, but they still need the same things, they just spend more on them. Instead of spending five pounds on something, they will spend twenty, or a hundred."

"I'd like to swap places with someone in the successful world for a day, just to check it's the same."

The therapist laughs.

"Like a *Wife Swap* type thing," Sylvie says.

"What kind of person would you like to swap with?" the therapist says.

"With you?" Sylvie says, then blushes and says sorry.

"It's okay. You don't need to say sorry. What do you think you would learn from a swap with me?"

"I'd learn what you really think of me?"

"I think you know what I think of you. I am honest with you in therapy."

Sylvie looks at her but doesn't smile. "I'd like to see how it feels to be you. I'd like to see how grown-up it feels. I want to see how you feel about your clients, see who your favorite client is. Then in the evening, I'd do whatever you do in the evening. Like . . ." she says, and pauses and smiles.

The therapist laughs. "You'd like to see how grown-up it feels to be me."

Sylvie nods. "I'd like to see how different it feels, mainly. It seems crazy that we can never know what it's like to be another person."

"Well, since we can't do a swap, the best we can do is try to speak honestly here in the therapy room and describe how it feels."

"Only one of us can do that," Sylvie says.

"I think it will still work," the therapist says, and she leans an arm behind her to pull the curtain over the window and the curtain goes over Butter's head.

"I had this book when I was little," Sylvie says, "where a girl swapped places with her dog, just for an hour or something."

"That's sweet. What did she do when she was her dog?"

"I think she found something that she'd lost. There was something of hers buried in the garden, and when she was her dog, she was able to sniff it out, and dig it up."

The therapist smiles.

"From what I can remember, she enjoyed being a dog and she felt really free. She didn't have to worry about the school bullies, I remember that part. But when she changed back into herself, she did realize how happy she was to be her, to be a human."

Butter nudges the curtain away with his nose and jumps down from the window ledge, then up onto the therapist's lap.

"I'm sure you'd realize how happy you are to be yourself if you swapped places with me, then swapped back to yourself again," the therapist says.

Sylvie makes a humming noise, then says: "Do you ever wish you'd kept a tally of days you were happy and days you were unhappy? So you could count them up at the end of a year, or at the end of a decade. I wonder why nobody is encouraged to do that."

"You could always start now," the therapist says, "if you wanted to do it. But I think it can be hard to judge whether you are happy or not on one day. Happiness usually comes just in moments."

"It wouldn't be exact. But don't you think you know, at the end of a day, whether you've had a good day or not?"

"I don't know if it's helpful to categorize your time like that: *have you had a good day, have you had a good weekend.* People do that, but . . ."

"Right," Sylvie says. "I really hate it when people ask me that. I guess I just want to know what percentage of my life I've been happy and what percentage unhappy."

The therapist nods.

"Then I could compare it to my friends and to every other person in the world," Sylvie says, laughing.

"And would that help you, do you think?"

"I'd be able to see how normal I am."

"But what is normal?" the therapist says.

"Right, I know, *what is normal,*" Sylvie says. "But also I'd like to know if humans, altogether, are happy for over fifty percent of the time. I just think we should know. I'm surprised we don't know."

"Do you think it would be helpful to know?"

"I think so. I feel like it would be under fifty percent, and I think that's bad. I think it would show that we aren't a successful species."

"I think for now, we should concentrate on you . . . on whether you are happy."

"But if you think of humans," Sylvie says, "if you just picture a group of them, together, not drunk, and then you picture, say, a pack of dogs together, you definitely imagine the dogs happier, their tails wagging. And if you picture the humans happy, you assume they are either faking it for the camera, or drunk, or on drugs."

The therapist smiles and Sylvie and the therapist both look at Butter on the therapist's lap.

"Dogs have a simpler life, I suppose," the therapist says, "with simple needs that are easily met."

"They just want food, a walk, and somewhere to sleep," Sylvie says. "Though actually, when I worked at the dogs' home, there *were* a lot of unhappy dogs. The ones that hadn't been adopted. So maybe they need an owner to be happy, they need someone in charge of them. Then they get looked after, like eternal children. And they have no existential angst."

The therapist laughs. "Right," she says, "no existential angst."

"They don't have to work out what to do all the time. The constant decisions. It's hard!"

The therapist nods. "Well, you do what's important, you do your job, looking after the cats and dogs so you can pay your bills. And you have your own dog to take care of at home. And then, once you've done what's important, you can work out what you *like* doing, and do that."

"You make it sound simple," Sylvie says.

The therapist smiles.

"I keep having this strange thought about Curtains—my dog. Since my dad died."

The therapist nods.

"I just keep feeling like I can see my dad in her. In her eyes, mainly. You know she's brain-damaged and her eyes are a bit strange . . ."

"Yes, I noticed that," the therapist says.

Sylvie feels an urge to laugh—the therapist noticed, she takes notice when she bumps into Sylvie outside the therapy room!—but she shakes it off and carries on. "Well, my dad's eyes went a bit strange too, with his illness. And sometimes I wonder if it's him, looking at me. Maybe he wanted to hang around for a bit longer, and that's how people do it? I know someone else whose dad died and then they had a similar experience with a dog, with a golden retriever."

"Really?" the therapist says. "Do you think it's possible?"

"I don't know. Nobody can know those kinds of things, I guess. But . . . I don't know why he would have chosen Curtains. She just walks in circles and pees in the house."

The therapist smiles.

"I suppose that could be why, though. Maybe he wanted to see how it felt to do these things but be accepted, or seen as cute. People think it's disgusting when humans can't control their body, their bodily functions. Maybe he was sick of the way people looked at him and he wanted to be looked at the way people look at Curtains. Everyone finds her adorable."

"Oh, that's sad for your dad," the therapist says. "It's a nice idea. Maybe, also, he wanted to spend more time with you, his daughter, and that's why he chose Curtains."

Sylvie smiles and starts to laugh. "Oh god. It makes me feel, I don't know. The way that we are talking about it as if it's a possibility. It makes me feel crazed, just the idea of it."

"That your dad could have gone into your dog, or that your dad might want to spend time with you?"

"I don't know," Sylvie says, "maybe both."

The therapist nods but doesn't smile.

"You probably picture my dad just floating in space, dressed as Hitler, counting down from ten to zero at the beginning of my nightmares, I know I keep talking about that. But I have some nice memories. Like when he'd bring

Chinese takeaway back on Saturday nights, and we'd sit on the floor in the lounge and eat it watching *Monkey*. Do you know it? *Monkey Magic*?"

"I don't!" the therapist says brightly, interested.

"It was really good, a bit scary, a bit strange. In the opening credits there was this big stone egg that started to hatch. And a voice would say: *The first egg was called thought*. I think Dad liked to start on his chicken balls at that part. We used to try to say the words to the intro together: *The nature of Monkey was irrepressible! With our thoughts we make the world.*"

"That's a sweet memory," the therapist says.

Sylvie nods. "I think it's a real one," she says.

23

A STAMP

SYLVIE HAS ARRANGED TO MEET CHLOE for a walk on Halloween. They meet near the bottom of the hill and walk up the road toward the therapist's house. It's already dark and they stop under a streetlamp to look at each other's outfits.

"I'm so happy we look the same," Sylvie says, glad that she got to choose their outfits, glad that Chloe agreed to it all. She notes how good Chloe looks in this outfit, but then reminds herself that most people look good in this outfit. Still, she thinks, Chloe looks particularly good.

"We look like boarding school witches," Chloe says, laughing.

They are both wearing a white blouse with a black cardigan, a black skirt, white socks and black shoes, a black coat, and a witch's hat with long synthetic hair attached. They carry on walking up the hill.

"I'm sorry about the therapist, I'm sorry she can't see you," Sylvie says, trying to keep up with Chloe, out of breath slightly.

"She's being very professional, saying she can't see both of us."

"She likes to stick to the rules. She likes the code of ethics . . ."

"It's disappointing," Chloe says, and Sylvie feels it too, she feels something worse than that, she feels the approach of boredom and she knows she could connect the idea of boredom to the therapist's behavior, to the therapist, but makes sure she doesn't.

"She seemed really disappointed too," Sylvie says. "She seems interested in you, she always leans forward when I mention you. I think she is impressed about how in-the-world you are."

"We're both equally in-the-world," Chloe says. "You and I. This is the world," she says, gesturing to the hill they are approaching, "as much as anywhere. I think the therapist should be encouraging you to see that."

"I think she tries," Sylvie says.

They reach the top of the hill and sit on a bench and Chloe puts her hand in her pocket and brings out a bag of Catherine Wheels and Sylvie gets a bag of Jelly Babies out of her bag. They open the packets and start to eat.

"It makes perfect sense that you'd bring licorice," Sylvie says, looking over.

Chloe smiles. "Did you know licorice can kill you? It can

mess with your heart, make your muscles weak." Chloe unravels a Catherine Wheel with her teeth. "And what do you have? Jelly Babies?"

Sylvie nods and puts three in her mouth. "I don't know what's in them, but they make me feel full in a way that nothing else does. Do you know what I mean?"

"I think so!" Chloe says happily.

"It feels good to be an adult," Sylvie says, "and not have to trick-or-treat to get sweets."

Chloe nods and unravels more licorice.

"I wonder what sweets the therapist likes best," Sylvie says.

"Cherry Lips?" Chloe says.

"God," Sylvie says, excited. "I also think she'd like toffee. The stuff you have to break with a hammer. The stuff that looks like a natural mineral, like rock, like gold. I wonder if the therapist has ever swapped sweets while kissing. I wonder if she's ever had a Gobstopper."

Chloe snorts. "Oh, look at the moon," she says then. They stand up to look at the moon, and Chloe gets out her phone and takes pictures of them both with the moon in the background, their two faces and the moon making three white circles on the phone screen. They adjust their witch's hats to make space for the moon.

"I never know what to do with my face in pictures of us," Sylvie says, wishing she looked better, wishing she knew how to eliminate the awkward affliction that smothers the visuals of her face, or that she knew how to eliminate her awareness of it, at least.

"We need to relax our faces," Chloe says. "Apparently, saying, *Yes, no, yes, no,* is the quickest way to do it."

Sylvie alternates saying *yes* and *no*, making exaggerated facial movements. "I don't think it works. It just reminds you how hard it is to be human. All the things you have to say *yes* or *no* to."

Chloe laughs, brings her phone down, and swipes through the pictures. "We both look much better saying *no*."

A dog barks and Sylvie turns to see a dog running on the grass, its white fur glowing in the dark. She grabs Chloe's arm.

"It's Butter," Sylvie says, trying not to move her mouth as she says it, and Chloe freezes in position like she's playing musical statues.

"It could be the husband walking him, remember," Sylvie whispers through her teeth.

There is a sound of someone clearing their throat, and Sylvie turns and is struck by the sight of the therapist, her face lit up by the moon. The sight seems to hit Sylvie's face like a stamp, multiple times. As if God has a stamp of the therapist's face, and is stamping it on Sylvie's face as validation, very quickly. *She is here, she is here, she is here.* The therapist is wearing a long black coat, and wisps of her hair rise above her head like a halo.

Sylvie puts her hand up in greeting, and she smiles and the therapist smiles back.

"Witches!" the therapist says brightly. "Are you going to a party?"

"No, we just dressed up for a walk," Sylvie says. She starts to play with the fake hair that is attached to her witch's hat and it starts to come out in her fingers.

"Well, you both look great," the therapist says.

"Has anyone come to your house yet?" Sylvie says.

"Come to my house?"

"For trick-or-treating." Sylvie blushes, but she feels sure it's dark enough for it to go unnoticed.

"Oh, no, nobody ever comes, though we always buy sweets, just in case."

"You have to put a pumpkin outside your front door to show you're taking part," Sylvie says.

"I didn't know that. That explains why nobody comes."

"Well, we won't come, we won't knock," Sylvie says, imagining the therapist's front door opening in the dark, imagining the golden glow of a single lamp, feeling an urge to lie down, imagining the therapist's fingers passing her a wrapped hard toffee.

"Okay," the therapist says, smiling gently. She turns around then and scans the green. "I've lost Butter," she says.

"I think he ran toward the turnout," Sylvie says. "Where the ice-cream van parks."

"Yes," Chloe says, "I saw him go that way."

The therapist thanks them and walks backward for a few steps with her hand in the air. Sylvie and Chloe put their hands up and both wish her good luck, and Sylvie imagines silver webs between each of their hands, joining them together in a triangle. When the therapist turns and walks away, Sylvie looks down for a moment, and she feels she will have to change her face to be able to look up at Chloe again.

"Wow," Chloe says. "Are you okay?" she says, and Sylvie looks up.

"I'm sorry," Sylvie says. "I don't know what happened."

"She seems really nice!" Chloe says, and Sylvie puts a

hand on her chest and wonders if she wishes the therapist were slightly less nice so that seeing her would be easier, and decides that she doesn't.

"Do you think she knew who I was?" Chloe says.

"I didn't introduce you," Sylvie says. "I'm sorry. My social skills are so bad."

"I mean, it was the therapist," Chloe says. "I don't blame you."

"Do you think it went okay?" Sylvie says.

"It went very well," Chloe says. "We bumped into the therapist dressed as witches, we ate sweets, her dog fled."

Sylvie laughs. "Well, and now she's smiled at you. How do you feel?"

"I feel exactly the same!" Chloe takes Sylvie's arm, and they start walking again.

"But do you know what I mean?" Sylvie says, looking over at Chloe, feeling desperate for her to have seen what she sees, but at the same time wanting to be the only one who can see it.

"She was taller than I expected," Chloe says. "And . . . she had the look of someone at a funeral?"

Sylvie starts laughing. "Did she?"

"The shape of her coat was exactly the shape of a coffin." Chloe draws the shape with her fingers in the air.

Sylvie thinks for a moment. "But isn't that because coffins are made to fit human bodies? Like . . . like coats are?"

"Right!" Chloe says.

Sylvie turns to look over at the therapist's house and she notices that her eyes are level with the therapy room, though the therapy room is on the second floor. She lowers her gaze and sees the therapist and her dog at the front door.

"There they are," she says. "She found him."

Chloe turns to look. "A perfect ending," she says.

They carry on walking, still arm in arm, silent for a moment.

"Did you notice that she didn't have a bag?" Sylvie says then.

"I guess her house is right there. Maybe she didn't need anything?"

"It's just, I *never* see her holding or carrying anything. But she somehow gives off the impression of having all the important equipment. And there's this feeling that everyone is waiting for her because she has all the equipment."

"The important equipment? Like what?"

"I don't know. The equipment for sports day, maybe? Or, I guess, the equipment for love?"

Chloe snorts. "What equipment do you need for love?"

"I don't know! I just feel like the therapist is carrying it."

Chloe laughs. "Shall we swap sweets now . . . just with our hands?"

Sylvie nods and takes a Catherine Wheel from Chloe's packet, offering Chloe the bag of Jelly Babies at the same time. Sylvie hates licorice, but she wants to be the kind of person who likes it.

24

IT'S NOT YOUR FAULT

SYLVIE IS IN HER FRONT ROOM after work, reading on the sofa that is marked all over with dots and dashes of ink. It's dark outside and she has the light on and the blinds aren't drawn, so people walking past will be able to see her. She likes having a possible connection to people outside, she likes imagining them seeing her as they go past—a girl on a sofa reading a book. They'd assume they were seeing someone with human feelings, enjoying reading about other humans with human feelings, because she feels like a human herself.

Sylvie hears footsteps on the street that sound like how the therapist's footsteps sound when entering the therapy room, so she turns off the light and goes up to the window. There's a woman over the road who looks similar to the therapist, but it can't be the therapist, unless the therapist has done something different with her hair and is in a rush. Sylvie hasn't seen the therapist in a rush, and this might be what her facial expression looks like when she's rushing. Sylvie tries to convince herself that it could be the therapist, but Sylvie's body isn't having the reaction it has when she sees the therapist, it isn't shaking, beating faster, sweating, out of breath. If she listened to her body, there would be no debate, there'd be no way it could be the therapist.

Sylvie switches the light back on and resumes reading. She is at a chapter where the narrator has had a long and confusing dream and is calling her therapist to talk about it. Sylvie stops reading and looks up from the book. This person is able to call her therapist, just like that, the moment she wants to talk to her? And the therapist happily goes along with it? Is this something that happens? Sylvie wonders if the character in the book is a special patient in some way—the therapist's favorite, or a famous person, a celebrity patient. Maybe it's a different kind of therapy—a more expensive kind. Because it seems like something that would happen in a different world than her world, it seems like something that would happen in the successful world.

Three days later, Sylvie looks up at tiny clouds while she waits at the therapist's front door; they are far away and look pink at the edges. Going up the stairs, singing, *One, two, three, shake your body down*, Sylvie feels bad that the therapist is having to talk to her for fifty minutes when she could be out in the sun with the pink clouds. In the therapy room, she watches the therapist pull the curtains halfway across the window. The therapist is wearing a gray jumpsuit and Sylvie makes an effort not to stare. She would never be able to wear a jumpsuit herself; she imagines wearing one feels close to the feeling of being naked, causing a follow-on feeling that she was going to start having sex at any minute. She tries to stop thinking about it as she watches the therapist putting their waters down on separate tables. The therapist sits down and asks Sylvie if there is anything specific she wants to talk about.

"I did want to talk to you about something that happened in this book I'm reading." Sylvie has brought the book to the session and she gets it out of her bag, but the therapist doesn't look at it or stretch out her hand to take the book, she keeps her gaze on Sylvie's face. The therapist never wants to look at evidence, it's as if she only wants Sylvie's subjective version of things, not the real, objective version. It's off-putting, as if the therapist isn't taking things seriously, as if she doesn't care about the truth.

"I just got to this chapter where the main character wakes from a dream and immediately calls her therapist to talk about it." Sylvie gives the therapist an incredulous look.

"We can talk about your dreams," the therapist says. "Of course. Is there a particular dream you would like to talk about?"

Sylvie doesn't speak for a moment. She doesn't know if the therapist has missed the point, or if she sees Sylvie's point very clearly but is making a more meaningful point by refusing to acknowledge Sylvie's point. She looks up at the therapist. The light is still bright behind her, despite the curtain being half-drawn, and the edges of her face aren't clear. Sylvie remembers then a dream she had in which the therapist had made an appearance. She remembered it upon waking, but then quickly forgot about it until now.

"You were in it," Sylvie tells the therapist, "only at the very end. At the closing credits."

The therapist nods.

"You came up to me and hugged me, but you only hugged half of me. Someone had drawn a line down the middle of me, I don't know who, a straight line down the middle of my face and my body, in black marker. And you knew you were only allowed to hug one half of me, and you managed it. You didn't go over the line."

The therapist smiles. "Did you think about what the dream might have meant?"

"I did wonder which half you hugged. I don't mean right or left, I mean the good half or the bad half."

"And what do you consider your good half?"

Sylvie looks down at her feet and moves the toe of her shoe backward and forward as if she is about to start a tap dance.

"Maybe the half that is humbler? The half that is happy with less."

The therapist tilts her head.

"I suppose I mean the half that is happy for you to be my therapist, and not the half that wants you to be my friend."

The therapist smiles. "I think it's okay to want to be friends with your therapist. I think a lot of clients want that. It doesn't make you a bad person. You know it's not a possibility, that the rules that prevent it are there to protect both of us, and to enable the therapy to have good and lasting effects."

Sylvie balls her fists and stretches out her legs.

"It could be that the line doesn't represent a split in you at all, a split of good and bad, or a split of anything. What about if the line just represented a boundary?"

Sylvie moves the book around in her lap, and then turns it over.

"We've talked a lot about boundaries. About putting boundaries in place with other people to protect yourself. And we've talked about the boundary in the therapy room. Maybe your dream was about this boundary and about what it means to you that I don't cross it."

Sylvie looks up at the therapist. "I do remember that in the dream I thought it was really skillful that you didn't cross the line, even by the tiniest sliver of a fingertip."

The therapist smiles. "I know you voice some frustration about the boundary—frustration that it prevents a relationship outside of therapy, prevents things like physical touch. But I think, really, you are very happy that the boundary between us stays in place."

Sylvie feels her smile getting bigger, tries to quell it, and puts the book back in her bag. She doesn't want the therapist to feel too good for being mindful of the boundary, she wants her to feel at least a little bad that she isn't giving Sylvie anything extra.

"I'm glad I managed to stick to the rules by not texting you during the week, by waiting for my session to talk about this," Sylvie says.

The therapist nods. "I'm glad too. This is one of the good things about being an adult—you can be in control now. You survived a controlling relationship, you are sober, and now you can experience what it's like to be in control of your own actions."

Sylvie nods and smiles. "It's such a good job I don't drink anymore. I would definitely be texting you nonstop whenever I got drunk."

The therapist smiles.

"I used to text people the same thing over and over. It was awful, I'd be like this," she says, and she mimes texting over a phone, her head tilted and tongue hanging out the side of her mouth. "I'd be like: *I think you should come over, I think you should come over, I think you should come over.* And I'd go through the texts the next morning and see when the person had decided to stop replying. I really do think people thought I was crazy back then."

"Well, you're not crazy."

"Or weird," Sylvie says. "Even my dad thought I was weird."

"You're not weird," the therapist says slowly, looking at Sylvie.

Sylvie looks at the therapist. She breathes in deeply, she is having the thought that she is nearly in the reality she wants to be in, she feels very close. She thinks she's having a thought and a feeling with the same content at the same time. When she looks at the therapist's face, she feels like she is going to cry and quickly lowers her gaze to the therapist's gray jumpsuit, looks at the folds of the fabric, looks at how it goes from her top to her bottom without stopping, without a seam.

"Can you say it again," Sylvie says, still looking down, "over and over, to help it sink in?" She looks up and sees that the therapist is smiling and she goes on. "Like in the film where Robin Williams is a therapist, and he keeps saying, *It's not your fault*, until the patient starts to cry. And when he cries, Robin Williams hugs him, and that makes him cry even harder—it allows him to let it all out."

The therapist smiles and tilts her head.

"It's the climax of the film," Sylvie says. "I used to watch it over and over."

25

SUGAR PAPER

SYLVIE IS ON HER WAY to London to see an author talk at the university, she bought a ticket for Chloe and has arranged to meet her there. There are two copies of the author's latest novel in Sylvie's bag, one for her and one for Chloe. A striped paper bag stands on the train table—Sylvie is trying to keep it pristine, away from her hair or dirt, or the dirt of other people.

Her phone buzzes, and it's Chloe.

Still in meeting. But I'll escape, she texts, adding a fingers-crossed emoji.

I'm so happy this is going to be our first evening out together, Sylvie replies.

Chloe replies with a heart.

When the train stops at Charing Cross, Sylvie inserts

herself into the flow of people. She feels like a cell joining plasma, which feels good, and she doesn't stop to wonder why she's moving through space from A to B. Out on the street, Sylvie looks up at the traffic lights, thinks how they glow much brighter in the city—all the lights do. Probably the brightness of lights controls the amount of possibility a human brain believes in, so they do this on purpose, to keep people trying harder in the city. People make the lights brighter, try to expand their brains.

Sylvie walks quickly in the dark, she knows the way, she went to the sister university when she lived in London with Conrad. It feels good to be back; she walks down Adelaide Street, down St. Martin's Lane past the ballet shop, across Shaftesbury Avenue past the umbrella shop, then she's in Bloomsbury and she keeps going, following people who seem to be thinking without doing any thinking herself.

On arrival, Sylvie gets stamped at the desk and goes straight to the toilets. She wonders if the author will use these toilets too, or if there are separate ones backstage. She doesn't want to encounter the author here, in the toilets, and have a conversation in the mirror like the scene in her second novel. Sylvie looks up when she washes her hands, sees her reflection looks flushed and excited, and leaves to find a vending machine. She wants the vending machine to absorb her nervousness by making her feel like she's in a teen drama, and it does, she feels good when she leans down to get the can from behind the black flap. She waits there for Chloe, half in the machine's shadow, leaning back against the wall, the paper bag between her feet on the vinyl floor.

As soon as Chloe texts, *I'm here*, the automatic doors open and she's there, rushing and happy. Sylvie feels like she's in the world when she sees Chloe, feels sure they are both in the same world, and walks toward her to hug hello.

"You made it!" she says, then slides backward to retrieve her paper bag. "I brought treats for the author," she says, almost whispering.

"That's so nice!" Chloe says, looking inside the bag.

"Probably everyone has brought her treats, though," Sylvie says.

Chloe laughs.

"I wanted to get her a cake but I didn't want her to worry I'd poisoned it and then not be able to eat it. So I got her things that were in completely sealed packets. Sweets, mainly."

Chloe laughs. "I doubt she'd worry about being poisoned," she says, and goes to the desk to register.

Chloe's cheeks are flushed when she comes back. "They asked if I wanted to meet her."

"What!" Sylvie says. "Why?"

"Maybe she recognized me from the gallery? I don't know!"

"And what did you say?" Sylvie feels agitated, she's not sure if she feels good or bad.

"I said: *No, but my friend does*," Chloe says, clamping her teeth together.

Sylvie laughs. "My god. And then?"

"That was it, the conversation ended," Chloe says.

In the lecture hall, they choose the second row and put their phones on their knees ready to take photos. When the author walks onstage, Sylvie gasps to see someone swiped away from the successful world and placed in this world, where Sylvie is able to see her. The author is wearing navy blue, and she looks slightly smaller than her author photos, but she's definitely here, functioning with no glitches. Sylvie and Chloe listen to the reading, they laugh at the story of the prince, and glance at each other as they laugh. When they go up to get their books signed, Sylvie presents the author with the bag of treats, remembering she'd also put sheets of sugar-paper rottweilers in there, because she'd read that was the breed of the author's dog. Sylvie is shaking and happy, and glad she can give the bag, then step back down to watch Chloe get her book signed. She watches with a hot face, amazed to see her real friend talking to her favorite author in the same time and place.

On the train home, Chloe opens her book at the title page to study the signature and Sylvie gets out a notebook and pen.

"You're writing! Has she inspired you?" Chloe says. She takes a photo of Sylvie, then leans over to see what she's writing.

"You're just drawing hearts and writing the author's initials!" she says, laughing, and Sylvie laughs and draws more hearts.

"I loved the reading, I loved the bit about pushing someone through your dirtiest parts, how that's the only way to find someone you can really love."

"I loved that part too!" Sylvie says.

"I'm so glad you invited me," Chloe says.

"Maybe we shouldn't go out together ever again," Sylvie says, "so this will always be our only outing. Because we won't be able to top this."

Chloe laughs, then turns the page in her book and starts

to read. The train hums and shoots through space and the strip lights are bright. Chloe turns pages while Sylvie draws hearts.

"This is genius," Chloe says, looking up between chapters. "I love her freedom. It's quite mind-blowing."

Sylvie looks at Chloe and smiles and nods, then looks down and draws more hearts.

"It almost makes me not want to try to write anything myself, it's so good," Chloe says, then looks at her reflection in the black of the train window. Sylvie looks at her reflection too.

"But she's not you, and you're not her," Sylvie says to Chloe's reflection, and Chloe's reflection smiles.

26

ETERNITY

WALKING TO THERAPY, Sylvie thinks about how short the distance is between her house and the therapist's house. She remembers a school friend trying to communicate her pain at being right at the front at a Nick Cave concert by saying: *So near yet so far.* Then she remembers watching a YouTube video about how the extreme right and the extreme left are closer than you think—the horseshoe theory, they called it. The horseshoe shape is good, Sylvie thinks, it has to be shaped like that so it can keep the evil in, as long as you keep it the right way up, that's how it works. But which is the right way up? Sylvie catches the reflection of her top half in a car window. It looks like someone has put a yellow horseshoe sticker over her hair, around her face—she has bleached her hair and looks like a different person. Sylvie imagines having a mirror in front of her at all times, maybe attached to a headband, so she could see that she looks like a different person and would then feel free to do what she wants without worrying so much about the consequences, since she is somebody else.

The therapist is wearing a loose white linen blouse, open at the neck, and gray jeans with a cream belt.

"You've changed your hair. It looks very nice."

"I've always wanted blond hair," Sylvie says. "Since school! I didn't do it to copy you."

The therapist laughs. "That never crossed my mind." She picks up a section of her hair and pulls it in front of her eyes. "I don't think mine is really blond. It's more of a mixture. There's gray, and . . ."

"Peach?" Sylvie says.

The therapist smiles. "Do you think? So how does it feel?"

"I like it when it falls in front of my face. It makes me think of Victoria sponge, and the sun, and the popular girls at school. But when I look in the mirror and see it framing my face, it doesn't look right at all."

"You probably just need time to get used to it."

The therapist's eyes look wet and she seems to be stretching the bottom half of her face, and Sylvie tries to work out if she is stifling a yawn. If she is, Sylvie thinks she's getting better at camouflaging her stifling.

"I'm still waiting to see if it delivers its promise of a better life," Sylvie says.

"You think blond hair promises a better life?"

"Maybe. But I always make the mistake of thinking things promise a better life."

"Can you remember the first time you felt like that?"

"I think the first time was when I started going out with Nick."

"So when you were seventeen, eighteen?"

Sylvie nods.

"Well, that's understandable. At that age, you're splitting away from your family, preparing to leave home, and you're looking at different ways of living."

"Right. I knew there had to be a better way of living than the way my parents were living, and all my friends' parents. And it was obvious that Nick knew what it was and that he was going to show me."

The therapist nods.

"It feels confusing that Nick's dead. I keep feeling like I need to check things with him, ask him: *What were we supposed to do, again? To get a better life?*"

"What do you think he would say?"

"I guess the things he always said. Things like, *Just let it happen.* But things didn't happen to me the way they happened to him. Crazy things seemed to happen to him every time he left the house. He'd come back from town with a copy of *Junky* signed by Jilly Cooper. The William Burroughs novel. It never made sense."

The therapist smiles.

"I remember Nick's mum came into his room once, and she asked about this book we were all reading. It was a novel, *And the Ass Saw the Angel.* It was kind of dark, but it wasn't that bad."

The therapist nods.

"She'd read bits and it had upset her, and she asked Nick why he read things like that, and he said, *Because it's true, and anything that's true is beautiful.*"

The therapist nods and smiles.

"I know it's teenage," Sylvie says. "I definitely had that teenage thing, of wanting anything to happen and not caring if it was good or bad. If it was bad it was more romantic, even."

"But you don't feel like that now," the therapist says.

"No. I guess I've had enough bad things happen now, I've felt the effects, and see they can last, and I know now it's not fun, and it's not romantic."

The therapist nods. "It's good to learn that. I think that's part of growing up. You often say that you don't feel grown up, but you can see from talking about this you're very different from how you were at seventeen."

Sylvie looks down at her socks and shoes. "I still love how concerned Nick was with whether or not things were 'true.' Especially when our parents seemed to care so much about appearances. There was this feeling of everyone being superpolite and clean, with the neatest gardens and houses you've ever seen, but, you know, the usual story."

"The usual story?"

"Of the neatest people having the darkest secrets, of things being generally not what they seem."

"Do you think that applied to your parents? That there was something dark going on under the surface?"

"I don't know. Probably not. I think it was just that all adults gave me that feeling. Maybe it was the eighties. Everyone seemed to be making sex jokes all the time. We had to watch Benny Hill, Kenny Everett—his character Cupid Stunt—then things like the 'dollies' on *Play Your Cards Right*. TV was so gross. And then the Wicked Willie books."

"I don't think I know them," the therapist says.

"I guess none of that was dark . . . it was just kind of . . . gross. I felt the darkness more when my sister was watching *Top of the Pops*. I used to get such a sick, scared feeling when I walked past the back of her head and saw her watching it."

"*Top of the Pops*," the therapist says, "really!"

Sylvie laughs a short laugh. "I'm such a baby!" she says. "Scared of everything!"

"You're not a baby, not at all," the therapist says. "Can you think what scared you about *Top of the Pops* at that time?"

"I think the dry ice . . . and . . . I was scared of the older kids. They looked kind of hysterical, trying to get in front of the camera, swarming round the DJ. But I mean, I was probably right about that, about the DJs, Jimmy Savile at least."

The therapist nods gravely.

Sylvie grimaces, then gets a mint out of her bag. "Nick seemed so pure," she says. "He had this thing about not putting up posters. I remember he really scoffed when he came back to my bedroom the first time and saw all my posters. He said if you liked something and you really got it, you didn't need to put a poster up to show other people you knew about it. You didn't need the accessories, the merch."

"Well, teenagers like to show each other what they like, to get accepted into a certain group, and posters might seem an easy way to do that."

"But it was like Nick was on another level where that wasn't necessary."

"I don't know about there being different levels. It sounds like Nick just had a lot of confidence; maybe he had more self-knowledge than most people at that age, so he did things his own way."

Sylvie nods. "My dad made me take my posters down anyway."

"Did he? What posters were they?"

"Just band posters of the Cure. I think he thought their music was leading me to the dark side. He came into my room once when I was listening to the B-side of 'Lullaby' and was furious."

The therapist smiles and sighs. "So you had your boyfriend telling you to do something to be more cool, and your dad telling you to do the same thing to be good," she says, making quote marks in the air for *cool* and *good*. "And did you do it? Did you take them down?"

"I mean, I had to. But I left a secret one up, on the ceiling, behind a beam where my dad couldn't see it. My favorite one."

The therapist smiles. "I'm glad," she says.

"I feel like that poster was making a promise of a better life," Sylvie says. "I can still feel it now, if I imagine the poster—this face coming out of dark leaves, looking upward. I still feel a massive surge of hope if I see it."

"I suppose you projected the sense of hope you felt at that age onto the poster, and those feelings are still attached to that image."

Sylvie nods. "Sometimes it seems strange that the Cure are playing the same songs. Because their songs felt like promises, but then the band is still playing them, thirty years later. It's like they're making the same promise, that there's a better world, but . . . they are still in *this* world . . . still making the promise."

"Well, we only have this world. Could it be that rather than promising a better world, they are finding a way to be genuine in the world we have? Which, for them, means writing and playing songs. Maybe just the existence of these songs, that you like listening to and they like playing, already makes the world a better world."

"Oh," Sylvie says. "I see what you mean." Sylvie feels her brain adjusting, and, like moving a fridge, she feels she should wait an hour or two before using it again.

The therapist smiles. "I think you could work out for yourself what a better life would look like. That could be a good way to proceed. Even if Nick were here, I don't think his idea of a better life would be right for you. You have your own ideas now. You always had. I know you weren't happy to take heroin, for example."

"I guess," Sylvie says, wondering if fear could be called an idea. But she'd been right to be afraid of heroin, it was the reason Nick wasn't here anymore. Sylvie thinks suddenly of the clips she likes to watch of Robert Smith at the end of a Cure concert, thanking the crowd. The way he bows, walks from one side of the stage to the other, puts his hand on his heart. She doesn't think she's ever seen anyone look so happy.

"It can feel easier to give your life over to someone else and have them make your decisions for you. But I don't think that will work for you in the long run. At some point you will want to make the decisions yourself, for your life to seem real and true to you."

Sylvie nods. She remembers the nights she used to walk round town with her best friend from school, trying to spot the goth twins they liked. She remembers how they would drape themselves, defeated, across the bench that overlooked the convent if their search was unsuccessful.

"We can discuss options here in therapy," the therapist says, "but you are the one making the decisions. And you've started working out what you want already by trial and error. By seeing what feels right for you."

Sylvie nods and then smiles. "I was thinking the other day about what I'd want to do for eternity if I had to make a choice. If someone asked me to choose one thing."

"Oh yes?" the therapist says, smiling.

"I'd choose to sit next to you, in the therapy room."

The therapist crosses her legs.

"I'd like to be in the therapy room, but the room would somehow be outside, and it would be really quiet. It would be sunny but with an occasional breeze. Everything would go really slowly. If there were bugs around, they would crawl really slowly, then fall into the cracks at our feet."

The therapist smiles.

"That's just how I imagine the scene," Sylvie says, laughing. "It sounds kind of apocalyptic now I'm saying it out loud."

"It does!" the therapist says brightly.

"We would be dressed in white," Sylvie says, "and though our chairs would start by facing each other at a nonaggressive angle, like in therapy, they would move super-slowly, with the sound of electric cars, and end up side by side, nearly touching, but not quite. If we were both chewing gum," she goes on, "and we wanted to take it out, we would stick it between the chairs."

The therapist smiles. "I can see how much you want connection," she says.

"Is that what it is?" Sylvie says.

"I think so," the therapist says.

27

NEVER THE SAME

THE BEACH IS CLEAR OF PEOPLE. Then Sylvie sees what she thinks is Chloe coming toward her on the pebbles. It's obvious that it is a friendly presence, she can tell by the shape and the way it moves. As the figure approaches, Sylvie plays the game where she tells herself she is sure it's Chloe, and then tells herself she's sure it isn't, and she watches the figure change as she makes her brain switch between the two. She watches it change shape and gender, she watches the clothes change into different styles of clothes, and sees how she feels. When there is no question that it is Chloe, she stops playing the game.

"You're blond!" Chloe says, smiling.

Sylvie blushes happily, knowing pink looks good with yellow. "I look like Victoria sponge, I know."

Chloe laughs. "You look like an angel. And has the therapist seen you?"

Sylvie smiles and nods. They start to walk toward the pier.

"Did she think you were trying to turn into her?"

"She said she didn't," Sylvie says. "Though . . . I am starting to feel a bit like, what's the point of listening to her at all?"

"What, why?"

"Just because, is it not all fake? If she has to be nice, if she has to practice unconditional positive regard—I've been reading about this—if she has to make out everything I say as perfectly normal, or perfectly understandable."

Chloe nods. "Right," she says.

"If she wasn't at work, she might say something completely different, she might say things that make me feel really bad. There might be insults, horrible thoughts, all being stored up in her brain, in the place between work and non-work. I mean, I've been really annoying. I deserve for her to be mean. It feels weird that she hasn't been mean yet."

"No. Why would she be mean? I don't think this is happening, this thing with insults." Chloe looks at Sylvie. "Is she helping you?"

Sylvie nods. "I don't know why I'm even saying all this. There's no way I'd stop going to therapy. I'd easily pay her fee just to sit in the same room as her for fifty minutes and not speak, just look at her. I'd pay double."

Chloe laughs. They have reached the pier, it's closed and has been emptied of rides and stalls. They both look through the padlocked gates as they walk.

"I had this idea when I first moved here," Sylvie says, "that

I could get a stall on the pier and take pictures of people in Pierrot costumes. I'd have a few costumes in different sizes and people would put them on and I'd take pictures of them. To make money."

"That's such a good idea," Chloe says.

"I don't know if it would be really good in reality or really depressing. I think it would be one or the other. Do you think it would be awful in reality? People would look nice in their Pierrot outfits, but probably not before. And they'd have to get undressed."

"Not necessarily. They could just put the costumes on over their clothes? If you got big costumes."

"Oh!" Sylvie says. "How do you think like that? So clearly!"

Chloe smiles. "You would have to engage with strangers, though, to get them to come to your stall."

"I feel like I'd be able to do that if I was dressed as Pierrot. And I'd have thick white foundation all over my face."

"Are you good that way," Chloe says, "with a costume?"

"I think so. I think it's why I wear the same outfit every day, so it's easier to remember how to act, so I feel like one person."

Chloe smiles. "You've done well to do that, to choose a uniform to help you perform continuity. I often feel like I don't have a developed-enough sense of self because I don't have a *look*."

"You have a look!" Sylvie says. "I know your look." They walk silently while she tries to think. "Your look is . . . Library-Hotel-Performance-Archive, I think."

Chloe laughs. "Well, thank you," she says. "Thank you very much."

Sylvie looks at Chloe's brown hair; she has the top part of it up in a ponytail, the rest is down.

"Maybe the dressing-people-up-as-Pierrots idea would be better left as an idea. It's hard to know what to do about actualizing something like that."

"Yes," Chloe says. "It seems better to live with the fantasy of something, for the main part."

"I think that might be best," Sylvie says. "And I don't think you can go back, back to the fantasy if you decide to try the reality, to check which is better. Because you will then have broken the fantasy."

"But what if the reality is a hundred times better?" Chloe says. "Maybe it's worth the risk of losing the fantasy to find out. And then you will have the memory of it forever."

"Do you think memory is better than fantasy?"

They start to walk down an alleyway, one side of which is covered in bits of broken glass that look like jewels.

"I think so, because you can rest easy that you actualized your fantasy?"

Sylvie tries to imagine having achieved what she wants, feels something coming, maybe laughter.

"Plus, you will be able to remember the physicality. With fantasy there's no physicality," Chloe says.

"I don't know if I even want the physicality," Sylvie says. "I don't know if it's ever nice, or good?"

"But you want the physicality with the therapist? Don't you? You've said you feel like you're going to die without it."

"Right." Sylvie starts to play with her bottom lip as they walk.

"Hang on," Chloe says, "maybe the fantasy *wouldn't* be ruined, if the reality was bad. If you tried the reality and it was bad, maybe the fantasy would just take over again in your brain and persuade you that the reality had been good!"

"What?" Sylvie says. "Maybe."

"And then you'd try to do it again," Chloe says.

"And maybe the second time it would be better," Sylvie says, feeling less stressed. "Just by repetition, it would be better. I always prefer things once I've done them again and again."

Chloe gets a pack of gum out of her pocket. "Really?"

"Sometimes I think I can only really enjoy something if I know it's going to happen again. If it's going to be a regular thing, the same each time. Like therapy."

"The recurrence of therapy seems good. The repetition, as ritual."

Sylvie nods. "Therapy is always exactly the same: the room is the same, she's the same, the time we meet is the same. I just, I keep trying to get her to agree that I can come for at least a year. I want to know the future sessions are there, so I can enjoy the present sessions more."

"And what does she say?"

"She says things like, *Let's see how we go*. Seems like such a mother thing to say."

Chloe laughs. They have reached the end of the alley and turn to start walking back, swapping places so Chloe is on the jeweled side.

"But what about scarcity making something more

valuable?" Chloe says. "So if you had fewer sessions, each session would be more valuable. Like the way people say that it's the fact that our lives end that makes them, whatever, precious?"

"Do *you* think that's how it works?" Sylvie says.

"Not really."

"Me neither. Though . . . I do wonder about boredom. I wonder why I don't get bored when I do the same thing over and over again."

"But it's never the same," Chloe says. "Because you are never the same. When you and I meet, even when we meet at the exact same spot every time, we always say different things."

"Right," Sylvie says. "And when you keep the stage the same, you can concentrate on the people and really study them. I guess that's why therapists are supposed to keep the therapy room the same every week: the chairs at the same angle, the clock on the mantelpiece, the tissues on the table . . . so you can both concentrate on doing *the work*."

They are walking past the part of the wall where the pieces of glass haven't been sorted into colors—the multicolored wall.

Chloe snorts. "I love how they call it *the work*. I can't imagine it ever feels like work to you."

Sylvie laughs and looks at Chloe and feels strings of sweetness rise inside her like party streamers from a can.

"Do you know what, though?" Sylvie says, and waits for Chloe to look at her. "I asked the therapist if we could have a session outside in her garden."

"What?" Chloe says.

"I was getting this feeling in the therapy room . . . of it all being a play, of it already having been written. I just thought if we had a session outside, just one time, it might feel more real somehow, as if it was in the real world."

"Wow. The therapist's garden. It sounds like a metaphor."

Sylvie laughs. "I think the light will be better. I'll be able to see her more clearly."

"And she's really letting you do it?" Chloe asks, as they come to the end of the alley.

Sylvie smiles and nods quickly.

Chloe puts her hand in her coat pocket then and tugs out a brown parcel, hands it to Sylvie. "I nearly forgot, I have something for you. For your bedroom."

At home, Sylvie takes the parcel up to her room and unwraps it. It's a Pierrot pillowcase, pink, ironed, and neatly folded. It's from the eighties, when Pierrot was drawn as a girl. Sylvie puts the case on her pillow and smooths it out, thinking: *She hopes to open shadowed eyes on a different world.* She lays her head down and closes her eyes and takes a photo and sends it to Chloe.

28

POPPIES AND NETTLES

SYLVIE IS WALKING to the therapist's garden. She is wearing an olive bomber jacket—jacquard with a leaf pattern—over her regular black and white outfit. The sun is behind a cloud, but when Sylvie looks up she sees that the cloud is very small. It will pass very soon, and there are no other clouds in the sky, and she hasn't brought her sunglasses. She bets the therapist will wear sunglasses, and when the therapist wears sunglasses, the shape of her face seems even more perfect, and Sylvie finds it hard to look at her.

Sylvie stops walking, tries to decide whether to go back and get her sunglasses, then sees a figure at the end of the road. She realizes from the shape that it is the therapist's husband. He is putting something in his car, something like a bag of cement. Sylvie worries that it will look like she's stopped walking because she was rendered immobile by the presence of the therapist's husband, by his power or good looks. So she starts walking again, toward the therapist's house and the therapist's garden. When she gets parallel to the therapist's husband, she sees that he's wiping dust from his hands and opening and closing different doors of his car.

The therapist opens the door to the house, smiling. She's wearing sunglasses. She motions to the path at the side of the house and puts her hand out for Sylvie to go first. Sylvie brings her arms in as she walks down the path to avoid the poppies and nettles. When she sees two identical garden chairs in the corner of the garden, she stops and turns around.

"Take either one," the therapist says, smiling.

Sylvie goes to the chair farther away, puts her jacket around the back of it, and sits down. The seat is metal and cold.

"It's a nice day." The therapist gestures toward the sky. "We're lucky."

Sylvie looks around at the trees bordering the perimeter of the garden, looks back at the therapist, and smiles. The therapist is wearing white trousers with a white blouse and a cream cardigan. Sylvie has the feeling that the therapist has worn this exact combination before. If she's right, it's the first time the therapist has worn the same outfit twice for Sylvie's sessions. Sylvie looks at the low white wall next to her where a black beetle is walking down a crack between bricks.

"I'm happy for us to try this," the therapist says, "therapy outside."

"I like it so far," Sylvie says, smiling, looking at the therapist's hair, trying to work out its color.

"I can't help being aware that it's reminiscent of the vision of eternity you were describing. But it won't be for eternity."

"I know," Sylvie says, smiling, and scrapes her shoes backward and forward on the concrete floor.

"There is something I have to tell you," the therapist says, and Sylvie's stomach pushes upward in her body like a plunger going the wrong way. She doesn't want the therapist to keep talking and she stays very still.

"I have to tell you that I'm retiring next year, and I'll be shutting down my practice," she says.

Sylvie's mouth dries and puckers up like she has reached ninety years old in less than a second. She pictures the scene in *Indiana Jones* where the wrong grail is chosen, in a flash. She looks away toward the garden gate.

"We still have a couple of months. I wanted to tell you now, so we have time to talk about it, and so we can make sure it is a good ending for you."

Large black oval shapes come into Sylvie's vision. It's as if parts of reality have been cut out, and she can see through them into space. She's seen a poster of an animal—a dog, or a horse—like this, with their face cut out . . . at Conrad's? Sylvie presses down on her eyelids and feels a layer of white pain surrounding her body. When she takes her hands away from her face she says quietly, "If we stop, it will be like none of this ever happened."

"That's not true," the therapist says, after a pause. "It will all be inside you," she says, frowning. "And *you* know that it's happened."

The therapist tells Sylvie that she will be back and she goes into the house, and when she opens the door, Butter runs out. He runs straight to Sylvie, jumps onto her lap, and reaches up to lick her face. Sylvie glances at the open doorway, then down at the dog. And even though she knows he's a dog, Sylvie leans down and whispers, "What on earth am I going to do?"

When the therapist returns, she places a box of tissues on the low white wall next to Sylvie.

"Butter came to comfort you," she says brightly.

"He's been licking my tears." Sylvie takes a tissue and blows her nose and rests a hand on Butter's back.

"How do you feel?"

Sylvie shakes her head. "I thought therapy would go on forever. Or I thought . . ."

"Yes?"

"I thought the long-term plan was that you were going to adopt me."

Sylvie looks up at the therapist and laughs and the therapist smiles and laughs.

"That wasn't the plan," the therapist says. "But we should talk about it. We are laughing, but . . . why did you want that? What would it be like if I adopted you?"

"I would just . . . never have to worry about anything."

"What would you stop worrying about?"

"Just, the important things. Like whether my life was good enough."

The therapist nods. "And why would me adopting you make your life feel good enough, do you think?"

Sylvie puts her balled-up tissue between her legs, then puts her hand back on Butter. "If I lived here with you, in this house, I think it would just feel like I was in a story, in a novel."

The therapist smiles. "What would happen in the novel?"

"Nothing much would happen, but it would never be boring."

"No?" the therapist says, smiling.

"It wouldn't be flat. Things would have meaning. There would be connections, and layers."

"Do you find your home life boring?"

"Not my home life *now*. I do what I want, I don't make myself do boring things, like go to the garden center or church or antique shops."

The therapist smiles.

"I think sometimes I just want to be with another person. But like how it is in a novel or a play, where nobody is afraid to say what they want, and they don't talk about an endless stream of stupid things, and it's not boring."

"And you feel like it would be like that if you lived here," the therapist says.

"Yes. I feel like I can say what I want with you."

"I'm glad," the therapist says. "But you know, this is therapy."

"I wish I could know what it would be like if it wasn't therapy."

The therapist nods. "Well, I am your therapist. This is how we've met and this is our relationship to each other."

Sylvie looks at the place where the therapist's white cardigan meets her white jeans. She feels, for some reason, that she needs to look for the remote.

"But you can experiment with other people. You can experiment with saying what you want with your friends and see what happens."

"I guess I already say what I want with Chloe. That happened naturally. It happened straightaway. I just, I wouldn't want to live with her, for her to get sick of me."

"I think it will be good for you to find more people like Chloe—people you feel comfortable, but not bored, with. But I don't think you need to be adopted by anybody. I think you're ready to embrace being in control of your own life."

Sylvie nods and sighs.

"Maybe a novel seems appealing because a novel has already been written," the therapist says. "All the decisions have been made. You get to just see things unfold. But in life, you *have* to face the unknown and make decisions. It can be hard, but that's what life is like for everybody. It's *all* the unknown. *Nobody* knows what is going to happen."

Sylvie stretches out her legs, Butter is still on her lap, and he loses his balance but steadies himself quickly.

"Making decisions about your life can be exciting," the therapist says. "It might feel uncomfortable at first, because you're not used to it—Owen was in control of what you did, what you read, what you watched, what you wore, where you went, who you saw. After years of living like that, you're just not used to having freedom."

Sylvie nods and strokes Butter. Butter strains to move forward and Sylvie takes her hand away and he jumps down. Sylvie brushes the white hair from her black trousers into her hand and puts it in her pocket. When she looks down then, she is surprised for a moment to see the metal legs of a garden chair, not the wooden legs of the chairs in the therapy room. Sylvie pictures the chair legs growing intricate black wings. She pictures herself and the chair on the cover of a children's paperback, flying up into blue sky with tiny white clouds. The chair would fly her back to her house so she wouldn't have to walk, she'd just tell the chair which house was hers, she'd shout it out while they were flying. Sylvie doesn't tell the therapist she is thinking this. She wonders if she will stop telling the therapist the things she thinks now, because the therapist will be going away, and all the things Sylvie tells her will be going with her.

29

VISIBLE SPECTRUM

WHEN SYLVIE GETS HOME, she lets her bag drop, then sits at the bottom of the stairs. She keeps shaking her head. She feels there should be someone with her, watching, to keep count of the shakes. Someone to decide when to take her to the hospital if the shakes get too frequent, if there aren't long enough gaps between them. Curtains is walking in circles at Sylvie's feet. Sylvie puts a hand out to stop her, and Curtains licks her hand.

What do you want from me? Sylvie says in her head. "Salt?" she says out loud.

She gets out her phone to text Chloe.

The therapist's dog licked my face today, she texts.

Chloe sends a heart emoji. *Nearly what you want*, she says.

I'd let any dog lick my face, Sylvie says, *but only one person.*

That's funny. Why so indiscriminate with dogs? Because they're a different species? So they're all the same to us?

And we aren't looking for a mate in them.

Chloe sends a thumbs-up emoji.

Maybe also because they're covered in fur so they're less offensive, physically, than most humans.

We bred them to look cute.

I've ordered a faux fur coat for therapy. I thought it might make the therapist want to touch me, if it's really soft.

Do you think you've been wearing the wrong uniform this whole time? You've been dressing like a student—strictly off-limits!

Oh god, maybe! Sylvie puts her hand out to stop Curtains from walking in circles again. *I keep thinking my dad has gone into Curtains*, she texts.

Chloe sends a coffin emoji, a broken heart emoji, and a dog emoji.

I actually googled "do dead people go into dogs." It wasn't a popular search. It kept suggesting "do dead people get eaten by their dogs."

Chloe sends a broken heart emoji.

I'm going to wear my fur coat for the Last Session.

The Last Session???? Chloe says.

She's retiring, Sylvie says.

No! God! I'm sorry!

I thought the plan was she was going to adopt me.

That did feel like the plan.

I don't know why I think I'm so special that she would adopt me. Why I always think I'm the special one.

You ARE the special one.

But this is the reality check. She's stopping practicing, and she isn't keeping me on. She's always talked about reality checks and now she's giving me one.

I bet she's going to miss you, I bet she wishes she could keep you on.

Chloe has to take a work call and says *to be continued*, and Sylvie puts her phone on the stairs and looks at Curtains.

"If only you could see what I see, with your eyes," Sylvie says to Curtains, not knowing what she means. She reaches down to wipe the hard crust from the corners of Curtains's eyes, then picks up her phone again and googles *what can dogs see*. Charts come up of *the visible spectrum of dogs* and Sylvie clicks on one. They show the range of colors a dog can see: blue, yellow, peach, and gray. Sylvie finds the chart beautiful and calming and she clicks on another, and it has the same effect. She keeps looking until her vision blurs, and then she realizes why the charts are so good—they contain all the colors of the therapist. The charts show the exact palette an artist would need if they were going to paint the therapist. Sylvie tries to get the words in the right order. The beauty of the therapist is the beauty of a person seeing a person as a dog would see them.

30

A DIFFERENT DOG

SYLVIE IS WALKING to the therapist's garden wearing a black faux-fur coat. When she gets to the wall that borders the therapist's property, she sees there is new graffiti there; it says BONE. Sylvie feels sick. What does it mean, why is someone trying to lay claim to the therapist's space? A crude face has been sprayed next to the words, wiggly lines coming off it like worms. Sylvie pictures herself coming back when it's dark to paint over it all with a large brush and thick white paint.

The therapist opens the gate. She is wearing a wax jacket, like the ones Sylvie's mum used to wear. The jackets come in blue and green; the therapist's is blue. Sylvie tries to remember which color her mum's was, and she switches between the two in her head, but both seem right. Sylvie takes the seat farther away, as she did last week. She leaves her coat on when she sits down and the therapist asks how she has been and how she's been feeling about therapy ending.

"I thought I was going to be able to see you forever," Sylvie says.

"No," the therapist says gently, smiling.

Sylvie doesn't smile.

"I'm not going to be here forever," the therapist says. "None of us are."

Sylvie swats a small fly away from her face. The therapist is wearing navy-blue wide-legged trousers; to Sylvie they look almost like scrubs.

"I'm sure some people go to therapy forever," Sylvie says. "They treat it like going to the hairdresser's. Hair never stops growing, it always needs cutting."

"Well, a therapist's aim is to make themselves redundant," the therapist says, "by giving clients tools to help them get through life by themselves."

"I bet Kate Moss and Madonna go every week, their entire lives."

"I don't think you need to do that."

Sylvie looks down at her feet and starts to drag the toe of one shoe around in a circle on the concrete.

"I can give you a couple of names of therapists that might be a good match for you, if you like."

"I'm hardly going to like another therapist."

"We still have a few sessions left. So we can make sure you have a good ending—I want you to feel in control of the ending."

"I don't feel in control at all. It feels like a game of musical chairs, and I'm frantically looking for a chair, but I know there isn't one for me, because you took it away."

The therapist tilts her head. "I'm sorry you feel like that. You know you can think about our sessions, the things we have talked about, whenever you need to. It could be like having an internal therapist."

Sylvie tries to imagine the therapist as an internal therapist. She pictures herself pushing Jelly Babies into the internal therapist's mouth with her tongue and smiles briefly, then grimaces. The back door of the therapist's house opens and Sylvie sees the silhouette of somebody moving past, and Butter runs outside. The dog runs around the perimeter of the garden but doesn't come near the chairs. Sylvie looks back at the therapist.

"It's just, this has been enough for me," Sylvie says.

"What do you mean, this has been enough?" the therapist says, her voice a little warmer now.

"Just, coming to therapy, to see you, once a week. I haven't felt the need for anything else."

"But you've been doing other things, therapy hasn't been the only thing in your life. You've made friends with Chloe. You've been doing well at work."

Sylvie pictures Chloe. She wonders if Chloe will miss the teenage obsessiveness, if she will find herself faced with a toned-down version of Sylvie, when Sylvie stops seeing the therapist. She notes with some interest that she is not going to share this thought with the therapist—it somehow feels more shameful and humiliating than all the other thoughts she has shared in therapy.

"But I can only tolerate the boredom at work because I know I have therapy coming up."

The therapist smiles.

"It's like you've given me this capacity for happiness," Sylvie says, "but it's in the shape of you, and nothing else will fit into it, so I won't be able to use it after therapy ends."

"I think you'll find that a lot of things will fit into it," the therapist says, smiling gently.

Sylvie shakes her head and brings her legs up to her chest and hugs them. She rests her forehead on her knees. She hears Butter sniffing around her chair and puts one hand down to stroke him, but when she parts her legs to look through them, she sees he has raised his lips and is baring his teeth.

"Oh, be careful," the therapist says, and pulls Butter away by his collar quickly. Sylvie pulls her hand up.

"I'm sorry," the therapist says. "I don't know why he did that. He turned into a different dog just then, I don't know what came into him."

"I thought he liked me," Sylvie says, trying to smile.

"He does, he really does. I'm going to take him in."

The therapist walks Butter toward the back door, leaning down to hold his collar and exposing her slim wrists. Butter stops to cock his leg on the garden wall, and looks back at Sylvie, and the therapist drops the collar for a second. Sylvie strokes the faux-fur of her coat with one hand.

When the therapist returns, Sylvie's cheeks are still hot. "Sometimes, I think I could say the same thing to you a million times, and I'd still need to come back the next week and talk about it again. And that's why therapy should never end."

The therapist nods and smiles.

"And I feel like I'm making everything up. Like I'm pretending that Nick died, I'm pretending my dad died, and my mum, and pretending that I was in that controlling relationship, all for sympathy."

"Your mind might be trying to protect you by telling you you're making it up," the therapist says. "But we both know that these things really happened."

"I still find it hard to believe I let that relationship happen."

"Well, you were constantly being persuaded, by the person you lived with, that their behavior was justified. Owen was using a whole variety of powerful techniques on you. It wasn't your fault. I know lots of intelligent women who found themselves in similar situations."

Sylvie nods and gets a mint from her bag. She makes a plan to think about the therapist saying *intelligent women* after the session. "I wonder if there's a magic number of times that I need to talk about it to really believe it happened."

"I don't think there's a magic number. I think you will reach your own kind of acceptance when you're ready." The therapist looks down at her hands, then starts to rub them together, and Sylvie thinks her face looks more pale and tired here, against the dark green leaves of the garden.

The therapist looks up at the sky. "It's getting dark, and it looks like rain," she says.

"What will we do if it rains?" Sylvie says.

"We'll go inside," the therapist says.

Sylvie imagines staying outside, watching the rain fall down on the wall that Butter cocked his leg on, washing it away, letting herself cry, her tears getting lost in the rain.

31

BIG

ON SATURDAY, Sylvie wakes on the edge of her bed. Her bed-room curtains aren't completely closed and sunlight falls in a long strip across her face. She props herself up on her elbows and stares at her pillowcase, then feels around on the floor to find her phone. She messages Chloe to ask if she's free.

Sitting in the driver's seat on the way to the beach, Sylvie feels that she loves her car, though it isn't the therapist's car, it is a much cheaper car and it is smaller and duller. She squeezes the steering wheel with both hands, then leans over to take a piece of chewing gum from the glove compartment; it must have been left there by Chloe.

Sylvie sees Chloe sitting by a big rock wearing sunglasses; she's raising her hand, waving. There are no clouds and the sun is making the sea sparkle—layer upon layer of jewels.

Curtains follows at Sylvie's ankles, on the end of a leash. Chloe has two cups of coffee propped up in the diamond shape that her crossed legs make and she hands one to Sylvie. When Sylvie sits cross-legged, her knees overlap with Chloe's. They both face the sea. Curtains starts to dig in the pebbles behind them to make herself a bed.

"I'm so glad you could come out," Sylvie says.

"I needed to get away from work," Chloe says. "I needed a different texture, from emails and Zooms. And it sounded more interesting."

"It's just a thought I had about the therapist," Sylvie says, "but . . . a completely *new* thought."

Chloe nods quickly, then shuffles in the pebbles to angle herself more toward Sylvie.

"I'm using the Pierrot pillowcase that you gave me and when I woke up, and opened my eyes, I actually thought it was the face of the therapist. On my pillowcase!"

Chloe laughs and widens her eyes.

"The therapist looks exactly like Pierrot," Sylvie says. "I mean, how Pierrot looked in the eighties, the female one."

"The female Pierrot. I *think* this makes sense," Chloe says, taking off her sunglasses.

"I've always liked how quiet she is," Sylvie says quickly. "I've always liked the feeling of being in the same room as her, but I could never work out what it was, the air she gave off. I thought maybe it was her beauty, or her status, or her age, or all three."

Chloe nods.

"But now I'm wondering if it's that she's been giving off the air of someone suffering from unrequited love."

Chloe sips her coffee and nods quickly.

"The way she walks, the way she sits, I always saw a regality in it, but maybe it's actually a kind of resignation, if she's quietly enduring great sadness. Maybe the silence, the nodding, the waiting, maybe it's not just a therapist thing, maybe it's a Pierrot thing too. So the reason I've been so attracted to her might be because she reminds me of the Pierrot figure, so I mean, really, because she reminds me of myself."

Chloe looks at Sylvie. "So it's been a self-affirmation thing as well as a masochistic thing, this whole time?"

"Yes!" Sylvie says brightly.

Curtains gets up behind them and turns around in the pebbles three times, then lies back down in the same spot.

"Do you want me to stop talking about her? Are you getting sick of it?" Sylvie says.

"No!" Chloe says. "It's not like we've resolved this. We still need to work out what has to happen to a fantasy for it to become . . . whatever it is that we want it to become.

"Is she still closing her practice?" Chloe says then, after a short pause.

Sylvie nods sadly, then suddenly grips Chloe's wrist. "Oh god. What if she's not really retiring, she's just saying she is so she can get rid of me?"

"No," Chloe says. "No, no, no. That's not what's happening."

"Imagine if she carried on having secret sessions with all her other clients in the basement, with a different haircut and a different name, once I've gone."

Chloe laughs. "That's definitely not going to happen."

Chloe looks at the sea and Sylvie lets go of her wrist. "I'm wondering, though, if she's a Pierrot figure, who does she have unrequited love for?" Chloe says.

"I don't know. It doesn't make sense. Who could reject the therapist?" Sylvie tries to call up an image of the therapist in an empty gray space, and not glowing or sparkling with light, but it's uncomfortable and she stops quickly.

"Well, who could reject Pierrot?" Chloe says. "Pierrot was the best one!"

"Right," Sylvie says. "I've never even thought about that."

"It's not about worth," Chloe says. "It hardly ever is. It's about power, it's about who's up and who's down."

Sylvie and Chloe both stretch their arms back to stroke Curtains. Stroking her at the same time, their hands overlap and they stroke each other's hands by accident, laugh, then pull their hands away quickly.

"You remember I was telling you how much I wished I could be the therapist's dog?" Sylvie says then.

"Ye-e-es," Chloe says, drawing the word out and smiling.

"So I could follow her around, live with her for the rest of my life, sit on her lap, be stroked by her hands, every day. So she'd love me unconditionally?"

"Yes," Chloe says, laughing.

"I was looking at these dog vision boards on the internet. They show what colors dogs can see. And it's basically the color scheme of the therapist. So if I was looking at her through a dog's eyes, she wouldn't lose any of her beauty."

Chloe puts her sunglasses back on and laughs.

"You're not going to be seeing her through a dog's eyes,"

she says. "You're talking like Christian Slater in *Untamed Heart*! When he doesn't want a heart transplant, in case it changes how he feels about the girl he loves."

"I used to love that film!" Sylvie says. "He's called Adam? And he thinks he has a baboon heart."

"Yes!" Chloe says. "He's so sweet in it. But the girl tries to get him to see that it's not our physical heart that changes how we feel. And I'm trying to get you to see that it's not our physical eyes."

Sylvie laughs. "It's neither the head nor the body," she says, looking at the sea.

"I think it's reassuring," Chloe says, "thinking it's something other than that, something bigger. Because then whatever we are might last longer, might last after our bodies die . . . might last forever, even."

Sylvie nods gravely, then she laughs, at the thought she's having that all she's looking at is shapes, shapes and reflection of light. She looks at Chloe, makes eye contact, and smiles.

32

A GOOD NURSE

ALL CAGES BUT ONE ARE OCCUPIED. Sylvie holds the clipboard. She asks the night nurse if anyone is due to go home and the night nurse says no.

"Try not to admit anyone else," the night nurse says. "We just don't have the room."

Sylvie goes to prep and makes sure the oxygen cylinders aren't empty or low. She attaches a giving set and mask to a cylinder and turns on the flow and breathes in the gas. She is sure it feels good, and she closes her eyes. One of the doors to prep opens and the head vet comes in and Sylvie turns off the flow.

"What are you doing?" he says. "Are you hypoxic?"

"I like to set up properly," Sylvie says, "and check it's all working."

The vet sits down at the computer. "You worry too much."

"Would you let me come here on my day off," Sylvie says, "if I felt like I couldn't breathe? I might be able to fit my whole body in the biggest oxygen tent."

"If you couldn't breathe, you'd go to hospital. The human one."

"But if the hospitals were full?"

The vet laughs. Sylvie starts to put away the instruments that have been sterilized. She reads the labels on the trays and puts each instrument in the right place. She realizes the vet thinks of her as a regular vet nurse who decided she wanted to be a vet nurse, then trained and took the exams and is now working as a vet nurse, doing the job she was trained to do, then she realizes that this is what she is, really.

"We might have a blood transfusion later," the vet says, reading the computer.

Sylvie quickly feels sick. "I don't know how to do that," she says.

"Nobody thinks they know how to do it," the vet says. "But it's simple, the first time."

Sylvie is kept busy and doesn't have time to look at her phone, doesn't stop for the toilet. When she gets tired, she tries to think about the therapist, tries to picture the calm world of the therapist's face. She's used to doing this instead of eating, instead of having a break, but she can't get the picture clear today. She keeps looking at the oxygen, wanting to breathe it in again, to make the picture stronger.

Sylvie is restraining a black-and-white dog on an examination table while another nurse applies a bandage to its front leg. Sylvie watches the neat movements of the nurse's hands, notices her glinting engagement ring. After a while, Sylvie rests her chin in the dog's fur.

"Have you ever breathed in the oxygen?" she says.

"No?" the nurse says, keeping her eyes on the bandage, concentrating.

Sylvie makes a noise.

"What color?" the nurse says then, holding up a selection of rolls for the final layer—red, green, and blue.

"Definitely blue. Dogs can see blue," Sylvie says, feeling happy that she knows.

Sylvie has been at work for eleven hours and has one more hour to go. She feels at home now. She feels love for the cages, the oxygen cylinders, the dangerous drugs cupboard. Three cats have just gone home and Sylvie starts to clean out their cages, removing their water, bedding, litter tray. When she wipes down the last one, she puts her head right inside the cage, lays it on the cold steel floor, and shuts her eyes. She wonders what she would feel like after eleven hours in the therapy room, if she was allowed to stay there for that long. Would she feel this slow and happy? Would she want to hug the chair, the clock, the box of tissues? She can't imagine feeling like that—eleven hours of therapy would feel more like endurance. A performance, like counting grains of rice, something to find your limits, see where you break. She'd prefer to be here at the vet's, where she's being told what to do, and where the point of what she's doing is always easy to understand.

Sylvie props her phone up in the cage and searches for the art video Chloe had sent her when they'd first met, the one she said worked as an exorcism. She finds a live version, where the artist is behind a desk and there's an audience. She presses play, turns the volume down, and wonders if she's had a good day. She's put bloods through the machine so many times that she feels she understands the logic of the clinic. She's getting better and better at finding veins, they pop up like magic, her eyes are sharp and her skin is glowing under the strip light. But would she prefer to be doing what the people in the video are doing? Would she prefer to be out of uniform, listening to the artist, joining in with the crowd, shouting, *Out, demons, out*? If someone else was playing her in the future, she'd prefer to be there at the show. But if she was playing herself in the present, she thinks she should be here, cleaning up after animals.

The door to the ward opens and the head vet comes in. Sylvie mutes her phone with one hand and makes cleaning motions with her other.

"What are you doing?" the vet says.

"Cleaning," Sylvie says.

"And how is the transfusion dog?"

"He's good. He's stable."

"Great. You did it. You knew what to do."

"I just had to monitor," Sylvie says. "Temperature, heart, and resps."

"The basics. That's usually all you need to know. You're a good nurse," the vet says, and Sylvie beams.

33

A PERFECT MIXTURE

SYLVIE WALKS to the therapist's house in her faux-fur black coat, she has her hood up. Someone has painted over the graffiti on the therapist's wall already with off-white paint. Sylvie thinks she can still see the letters BONE through the paint, but maybe it's just that she knows they're there. The therapist opens the garden gate wearing a long padded black coat and black gloves. She keeps her coat zipped up for the session and Sylvie doesn't see what she has on underneath.

"How have you been this week?" the therapist says, when they sit down.

"Good. I saw Chloe," Sylvie says. "She's putting on a show soon, she's going to get me a ticket."

"That sounds like fun."

"It'll be nice to watch a show, I think."

When Sylvie had searched for pictures of the performers online, she'd been excited to see that one of them had a similar look to the therapist—tall, slim, long straight hair, serious expression.

The therapist smiles.

"It's at the place I had my first date with Sandy too," Sylvie says.

"Will that be nice for you?"

"I think so. I remember the date so clearly. I remember standing next to Sandy on the escalator; as we went up, I remember looking down and seeing my thin gray socks and white slip-on shoes with little pink bows. Then when we reached the top of the escalator there was a pram, with doll's legs coming out, and white socks and black shoes. That was the start of the show."

The therapist smiles. There are a few moments of silence and Sylvie feels a fast panic that she hasn't felt before in therapy. She thinks the words, *It's over*, and wonders if the therapist will suggest they stop their sessions sooner if she has nothing left to say.

"Is there anything you want to talk about?" the therapist says. "I remember last week you said you could talk about the same thing over and over and still need to talk about it the next week."

"Yeah. I don't feel like talking about Owen today, though. Maybe I hit the magic number. Maybe I've finally accepted it happened now, the coercive control."

"It sounds like you've made progress," the therapist says happily. "We don't have to talk about Owen today. We can talk about whatever you feel like talking about."

"I'm more worried about the future than the past. I'm worried I won't find anyone I like the way I liked Sandy."

"You have lots of time to meet someone new," the therapist says.

"I'm not that much younger than you!" Sylvie says, then starts to blush. "I just keep thinking, what if Sandy was the one?"

Sylvie pulls her hands up into her coat sleeves.

"You're putting yourself under a lot of pressure if you think there is only one person for every person. You could try just going on one or two dates and see what happens?"

Sylvie worries that the therapist is as indiscriminate as everybody else seems to be, that she doesn't understand that Sylvie doesn't like other people, wouldn't be able to find one or two people she thought worth dating, especially after being with Sandy.

"Sandy was just perfect," Sylvie says. "A perfect mixture."

"A perfect mixture of what?" the therapist says.

"Of everything. Of inside the world and outside the world."

"How so?"

"He was definitely in the world, in his job, and I always felt like I was at the center of the world when I was with him. But he was also outside the world in the best way. I mean he felt shame at how people behaved in the same way that I did."

The therapist nods. "The center of the world sounds like a good place to be. But really, are you not always at the center of your own world?"

"I wish it felt like that. That's the dream, to feel like that. But I feel more like I'm living at the edge of the world."

The therapist smiles.

"I feel okay here. I feel happy we live on the same street. But are you moving? Away?" Sylvie feels a tight, sick tug of shame, knowing she shouldn't be asking, knowing she's crossing the line, but trying to pretend she doesn't realize she's doing this, so she can ask.

The therapist looks at Sylvie. "I'm not sure of my plans yet," she says.

Sylvie looks down. "I was sobbing the day you told me you were retiring. In my car. I was keeping it in during the session."

"You were keeping it in?" Sylvie thinks she can see pride and happiness behind the sad face the therapist makes when she asks. This is how Sylvie had hoped the therapist would feel, this is why she'd told her.

"I didn't realize at the time—that I was holding it in. But then in the car it came over me all of a sudden. I started making weird sounds like the animals make in the zoo in the middle of the night."

The therapist smiles. "I'm sorry," she says.

"Me and Sandy sometimes drove to the zoo at night. We'd park outside and put our seats down and listen."

"That sounds nice. Were you thinking about Sandy too when you were crying in your car?"

Sylvie tilts her head for a moment and then nods. "I think I was thinking about how inevitable it all felt. I was thinking maybe this is why I've been sad all my life, because I knew this ending was coming, like I knew the ending with Sandy was coming. I feel like someone must have shown me a slide-show, when I was little, of the endings of all these things, and that's why I've always felt so miserable."

The therapist smiles. There is silence again, and a car drives past.

"I don't want it to end!" Sylvie says, feeling a violent impulse for the first time in therapy, wanting to shake the therapist's chair by its legs.

"Well, it is what it is," the therapist says, after a pause.

"What do you mean?"

"Just—it is what it is."

"I don't understand what that means," Sylvie says.

34

A GOOD TIME

SYLVIE WALKS past deep queues of people to find Chloe. Chloe is standing in front of a thick red rope. She's wearing a blouse with a bow and a black shiny blazer, and her hair is glossy and falling down gracefully. She's smiling and holding a clipboard.

"You made it!" she says when Sylvie approaches.

"You look so nice!" Sylvie says.

"So do you," Chloe says, and gestures to the pleated collar of Sylvie's white shirt.

"We're in our in-the-world clothes," Sylvie says, and Chloe laughs.

"Do you want to go in now? I can let you in now, quickly?"

The lights are bright and Chloe has a walkie-talkie attached to the pocket of her blazer.

Sylvie nods and Chloe unclips the rope. "I'll find you later," Chloe says, touching Sylvie's arm as she walks through.

The room past the rope is darker, and Sylvie tries to picture the therapist standing next to her but it seems too impossible to imagine, even with the dark colors and strange sounds, and people from the successful world moving all around. She wonders if people would think they were mother and daughter, or a couple, if they were here together. Nobody would think they were a couple, Sylvie thinks, unless they saw them holding hands, kissing, touching each other's hair.

The music playing sounds like outer space. The floor is black and shiny and Sylvie feels that she could walk through the floor, going down softly, and thinks that might be a nice way for her life to end. She stops in front of a sculpture— there are black, red, and white bandannas piled into a mountain, the patterns and logos fast and familiar. It feels like Nick's basement. She remembers the time Nick pulled all his clothes out of his closet, heaped them in a pile, then dragged her over the heap and into the empty closet. She remembers it was dirty.

Sylvie sees some of the performers moving slowly, carrying a mattress together as if it were a coffin, as if this were a ceremony. They are wearing black and some look more male than female and some look more female than male but some don't look more one than the other. Sylvie's cheeks are hot and she looks around and can hear the sounds of alarms, but somehow they sound nice here. She gets a bottle of Coke out of her bag and drinks from it every now and then. She gets the sense that this is better. She tries not to think, *Better than what?* but she knows that if Chloe asked, she would say, *Better than therapy*. The performers seem to be able to straddle *both* worlds, the successful world and the unsuccessful world, in a way that seems . . . better. Sylvie would come here every week, she would watch the show every week if they put it on, if they had a residency and did this same show forever, but she knows that's not how these things work. But if it did work like that, she thinks this would be enough for her.

Sylvie sits on the black floor with her back against the wall and she parts her legs and looks down. She can make out her face, reflected in the floor. When she looks up she sees performers walking around at a different pace than the rest of the crowd. They are holding microphones that look black and heavy but they aren't using them, they are holding them almost like divining rods. Sylvie stretches out her legs and drinks more Coke. Someone else is sitting on the floor to the side of her, she sees their black shoes and white socks, and when she looks over they get up. They move seamlessly like a dancer, their gaze fixed straight ahead. They have a phone in their hand and Sylvie watches as they open their mouth wide and put the phone inside. It goes more than halfway in while she is watching. Sylvie notices Chloe then, standing by the opposite wall, flanked by a tall man and a tall woman, both with white-blond hair. Chloe says something to both of them, then walks toward Sylvie, smiling. Sylvie stands up.

"Do you like it?" Chloe says. "Are you having fun?"

"I love it," Sylvie says. "I'm so happy." She stands on her tiptoes for a second. "It feels like Nick's bedroom, but more . . . expansive."

Chloe laughs. "That's so nice! I'm glad," she says. "It does feel like a teenage bedroom."

"The dancers keep licking their hands and, I think, the pillars," Sylvie says.

Chloe laughs. "I know! I wish I could stay with you. I have to keep checking everyone, everything. I have to see how it's all going."

"It's okay, I'm fine, I'm really super-happy," Sylvie says, and she licks her hands and then takes a drink of Coke and smiles and Chloe puts her hands in her blazer pockets and laughs.

Sylvie stays for three hours, looking at the performers as much as she wants, knowing they are fine with her looking, going to the toilet when she needs it, drinking Coke. A few times, she spots the tall long-haired performer who reminds her of the therapist, and seeing them makes Sylvie feel especially centered and full. On her way out, Sylvie passes the poster for the show and stops to take a picture of herself beside it. She dips her head, pulls down her hair, to try to look like she could fit in with the performers, but she can't get it right. So she opens her mouth wide and puts her phone as far into her mouth as she can fit it, and takes a picture like that.

On the train home, Sylvie feels glad the train is full, but she's careful not to look around in case the sight of specific people makes this feeling stop. She picks up her phone to message Chloe, then hesitates, imagining her out for dinner or drinks with her colleagues and the performers. They will be sitting at a long table—Sylvie pictures the scene as an oil painting in deep thick browns and grays. Chloe would be at the head of the table, or hovering above it, her gold halo lighting up the room.

Sylvie has the feeling that she's balancing on a step, and she feels comfortable and happy because the step is right outside her house but also in the middle of everything. Maybe if she does message Chloe, the feeling will stay with her longer.

I had such a good time, Sylvie texts. *I liked the grey and yellow paintings and the bandannas and the movements. And the eating of the phones.*

Chloe messages back straightaway with emojis, a gray heart, a yellow heart, and a phone.

The whole thing felt so dignified. I felt full up, content watching them.

I'm so happy you could come.

Sylvie looks away from her phone and turns toward the window. She sees the reflection of her face hovering over dark buildings. She presses her forehead onto the glass, looks at the reflection of her eyes, then turns back to her phone.

I hope I can make this feeling last, I want to feel this good in my last session.

The Last Session, Chloe texts, and sends an emoji of a table. *Is it soon?*

It's next week! Sylvie replies.

I should be around more, now this crazy show's over.

Okay, Sylvie says, and sends a skull emoji and a mirror emoji.

Chloe sends a heart with a bandage emoji, then Sylvie puts her phone down on the train table and closes her eyes.

35

IMMACULATE

THE SUNGLASSES LOOK IMMACULATE. Sylvie puts them back in their case, holding them at the edges, careful not to spoil them with her fingerprints. She wraps the case in brown paper, kisses the package, and sets off to the therapist's garden. She can feel the blue sky very deep inside her eyes, like she's at the center of the universe.

The therapist opens the gate and Sylvie walks toward the chairs. When she trips on a flagstone, then recovers, her shoes make the sound of "On ne change pas," a song she'd been singing with Chloe after they watched *Mommy* at the same time. The therapist sits down and crosses her legs and smiles brightly. There is a plate of cookies balanced on the garden wall next to Sylvie.

"Our last session!" the therapist says.

She is wearing a blouse that is shiny, maybe silk or fake silk. Multicolored, it's brighter than anything Sylvie has seen the therapist wear before. Sylvie has the feeling that their last session has already been recorded and is about to play out. She wonders if it was a good session and if she had said all that she wanted to say. Maybe she has a chance now to change the script, if there was something she had forgotten to say, if she was able to make herself think, if she could somehow get her brain going.

"What would you like to talk about?" the therapist says.

"I feel like we can't really get into anything when it's the last session," Sylvie says.

"We can talk about whatever you want to talk about," the therapist says brightly.

"I did have these two things written down to tell you, but they never seemed to come up naturally, in a session."

"Okay. Shall we start there, then?"

Sylvie nods. "They are small and bitty. They both have to do with body parts of men."

The therapist nods.

"The first one was with my tutor at college. Just this weird thing he did with his foot. He asked me up to his room after a lecture because he wanted to show me his writing. He read me an awful short story about a woman walking really slowly out of the sea. I said I liked it, and then he stretched out one leg—he was the yoga teacher too—and stuck his foot up underneath my chair and wiggled his toes around, underneath me, where I was sitting."

The therapist frowns.

"I remember thinking he must have taken the stuffing out of the chair expressly for this purpose, because I could easily feel his toes. The second one was this thing that happened when I kissed my friend from college. I shouldn't have done it because he had a girlfriend, but he'd always liked me, and I guess I loved him in a way. I was trying to take the next step. I imagined telling people afterward: *We started off as friends, I never dreamed he was the one until I kissed him.* But the day after we kissed, these huge lumps came up around his ankles. It didn't make sense. It felt biblical. He called me to tell me, and I said, *I don't know what to say, I don't ever get lumps come up on my ankles, I don't think it's a thing.* I think we decided he was allergic to me."

Sylvie has the feeling then that she's told a fairy tale, like the tale of the three little pigs, a tale that has been told again and again by every generation, a tale everybody knows. She hadn't noticed if the therapist had said anything in response to either story and wonders if she will be able to access the recorded session to check, though she knows no recorded session exists. Sylvie looks over at the tall house across the road and sees there is a white dress hanging in the window, on the top floor.

"So do you think I'm okay now?" Sylvie says, trying to move away from the fuzz of confusion. "Do you think I'm okay therapy-wise?"

The therapist smiles. "You have really come so far since your first session. You are able to articulate your feelings more and think about where they might have come from. You are able to pause and see other options when you have an overwhelming reaction to something. You've made a good friend. You have more confidence. How do you feel about where you are now?"

"I don't know," Sylvie says, feeling it could also be true that her head is in exactly the same place as when she had come to see the therapist that first time.

"Is there no test to see if you're done? Do I not get a certificate, a patch, or a rosette?"

"No, there's nothing like that," the therapist says, smiling.

Sylvie feels that she needs to yawn but she doesn't, she keeps her mouth closed and keeps her breathing steady.

"I've been thinking about something different when I go to bed recently," Sylvie says. "I used to think about people that I liked," she says, looking at the therapist, "but I made an effort to stop. And now I think about words, but I think of them in 3D. Like I think of the word *HELP*. I imagine it standing up, in capital letters, and I try to work out which part I'd most like to fall asleep in."

"That sounds like a very nice way of self-soothing," the therapist says.

"I usually decide on the top of the *H*," Sylvie says, and she remembers that letter standing by itself, bright red, on the cover of a paperback she had once. "We were going to have the song 'Help!' at my dad's funeral," she says. "But I think we were all horrified at the idea of a person still needing help when they were dead."

The therapist nods and smiles.

"Are you going to move away?" Sylvie says when she can feel that time is nearly up. She looks over the road after she asks and sees that it isn't a dress hanging up in the window, it's a jumpsuit. She looks back at the therapist and the therapist isn't speaking, and Sylvie wonders if she missed what she said, or if the therapist didn't answer the question. Sylvie takes the present out of her bag and passes it to the therapist, and the therapist takes an envelope from between the pages of her diary and she starts to hand it to Sylvie, stopping to try to remove a stray hair that has been trapped at the seal.

"Don't," Sylvie says, assuming it's the therapist's hair. "I'll keep the hair."

The therapist doesn't laugh and Sylvie wonders if she heard her. She opens the card quickly, then watches as the therapist opens her present.

"I nearly got you Versace ones, but you know their logo is Medusa?"

"Is it?"

Sylvie nods. "And . . . I didn't want you to think I was suggesting you should get punished for your beauty, or anything like that."

The therapist smiles. "That wouldn't have crossed my mind." She takes the sunglasses out of their case. "These ones are lovely. Thank you very much. And I only got you cookies. Will you take some home with you?"

Sylvie nods. "Maybe I'll glaze them with something industrial so I can keep them forever."

The therapist smiles.

"I'm kidding," Sylvie says.

"I know," the therapist says.

When fifty minutes have passed, Sylvie feels herself starting to rise off the floor, to float, almost. She notices that the therapist is standing up and she thinks: *Out of nowhere*.

"We can hug goodbye," the therapist says, "since it's our last session."

Sylvie struggles to keep her head up, her eyes fall down to look at a crack in the patio. She didn't think a hug was in the cards and feels unprepared. It occurs to her that she doesn't have equipment for this with her, though she knows no such equipment exists.

"If you want to," the therapist adds.

Sylvie nods quickly. "Butter isn't here," she says.

The therapist looks around the garden, and then scans the windows at the back of her house.

"I'm sorry. You wanted to see him? I don't know where he is. I'm sure he'd have wanted to see you too."

Sylvie stands up slowly and heavily and moves toward the therapist. She's not sure if it is her who puts her arms around the therapist or if it is the therapist who puts her arms around Sylvie, but somehow, they are in a hugging position, and the therapist is taller. The therapist says something during the hug, but Sylvie doesn't hear what she says, and she doesn't say pardon, and then the hug is over.

The therapist offers Sylvie the cookies, holding them out toward her on a plate, and Sylvie takes two, quickly because she's shaking, and turns to go. She has the feeling that her face is almost inside out, preventing her from smiling. She walks toward the gate feeling a great urgency. She thinks she hears the therapist's voice say, "I'll miss you," but she doesn't look back or say anything in return. She concentrates on opening the garden gate, she keeps looking down, keeps walking. She walks past the tall house opposite that has something hanging in the top window but she keeps looking down, she doesn't look up at the window to see what it really is.

36

DISSOLVING

SYLVIE GETS STRAIGHT INTO HER CAR to see Chloe without going home first to pick up Curtains. The sounds of the waves on the beach are punctuated by the sound of flagpoles clanging.

"She hugged me," Sylvie says, sitting down at Chloe's feet so fast that pebbles fall into her shoes. Sylvie gets the feeling she said the words in the wrong order or spoke a different language, but she can tell from Chloe's face that she heard and understood.

"And I didn't feel anything," Sylvie says, putting both palms up in anguish.

"It's okay," Chloe says. "We know what this is. This is the fantasy-reality divide."

Sylvie looks at Chloe desperately.

"We could have predicted that this would happen," Chloe says.

"We could?" Sylvie says. "The fantasy-reality divide. Of course." Sylvie leans forward and digs her fingers down into the pebbles.

"Tell me what happened."

Sylvie sits up straight to speak. She says, "I feel like my face is dissolving." She covers her face with her hands, pressing her fingertips all around it, as if to prop up its foundations. "I can't believe my fantasy hug made its way into reality, and I missed it."

"The expectations were way too high for that hug."

Sylvie nods. "It felt like the difference between life and death. It was the only thing I wanted for months, nearly years."

Chloe nods in time with the beat of the flagpole.

"She said something when we were hugging, but I didn't hear what she said."

"Did you say pardon?"

Sylvie shakes her head. "How could I have missed it! What could she have said?"

"*Good luck for the future?*" Chloe says.

"*It will all be okay,*" Sylvie says.

"*You were my favorite client,*" Chloe says.

Sylvie smiles and her mouth trembles.

Chloe goes to get them both coffee and Sylvie gets the feeling of having nothing to do but wait, the feeling she only ever gets in hospital waiting rooms. It's just what she needs to feel, and she takes a breath that shakes her whole upper body. She stretches out her legs, then goes into her bag and brings out the envelope. When Chloe returns, Sylvie is staring at the therapist's handwriting with her mouth slightly open.

"Oh," Chloe says, when she sees the card. "Do you want to read it to me?"

Sylvie nods and dabs her eyes with the sleeve of her cardigan. "It says: *Thank you for being such an honest and open client. It has been a lovely journey, watching you grow into the person that you are now.*"

"That's very nice," Chloe says, handing Sylvie a coffee.

"I know. Don't you think it seems like a standard message, for any client? I thought it would be more personal, more intense." She puts the card back in the envelope.

"Well, we have nothing to compare it to. But don't forget, she can't let on that you're a special client. She still can't do that, even now it's over. And she's never been intense," Chloe adds, after a short pause. "She's never shown intensity, she's always been sensible, by-the-book, on an even keel."

Sylvie looks out at the sea. "What will I do without my weekly dose?" she says. "I don't have anything in place."

"Can you do something nice for yourself every week?" Chloe says.

Sylvie turns to stare at her blankly. "Like what?" she says. "The only activities I can think of that could trump the intensity of the pain are cutting myself, or some kind of drugs, if I can find drugs I'm not scared of."

Chloe's face falls. "You can't do either of those things," she says.

"I don't know," Sylvie says. "I feel I'm in an unbearable state. Like I need to work out how to die without dying."

Chloe frowns. "You know you're better than the therapist,"

she says. "You know you wouldn't want to cut yourself over her, if you actually knew her."

Sylvie shakes her head, then digs a hole in the pebbles to put her coffee in and brings her knees up to her chest, wraps her arms around them.

"Or what about concentrating on living with fantasy as fantasy?" Chloe says. "Even if the connection to reality has been broken."

"What do you mean?" Sylvie says, looking at the sea, feeling hope again, feeling confidence in Chloe's ability to show her ways of thinking that are less painful than Sylvie's default way of thinking.

"It was a fantasy before, and it can stay a fantasy now. You don't have to drop it. You can still daydream about getting together with her."

"Oh, maybe," Sylvie says. "Do you think that's enough? Even though it's not a possibility anymore."

"Was it ever a possibility, really?" Chloe says.

Sylvie starts to gnaw at her knees with her teeth. Then she stops and looks up at Chloe. "What is it about her?" Sylvie says. "What's the thing she's got that's been keeping me alive?"

Chloe looks at Sylvie silently.

"You've met her," Sylvie says, some pleading in her tone.

Chloe nods. "She was very nice. And beautiful. But . . . from the things you say, about what she says in therapy, she doesn't sound that interesting."

"But that's just because she's at work. She has to say all those things."

"Maybe," Chloe says.

Sylvie thinks about Chloe's colleagues at the gallery then.

Probably most of them are interesting, and that's what Chloe is used to. Sylvie might have developed low standards in interesting people, because of being with Owen for so long, because of working at the vet's.

"I just feel like after sitting in the same room as the therapist, just the two of us, with her saying these stock phrases and me saying the same predictable things over and over, I feel like I know her in a special way."

Chloe nods. "I do get that. But . . . because she can't give anything away, can't say anything personal, she's a blank canvas, you know? You can project anything onto her."

"But there's this special air she gives off that's bigger than anything she says or doesn't say," Sylvie says.

"Could it be that the special air is actually coming from you, not from her?"

"But I only feel it when I see her."

"It still could be something inside you, but she's just . . . activated it, for some reason. And you now need to find another thing to activate it. Or maybe it's a onetime activation type of thing and you won't even need it to be activated again."

"I feel like it definitely needs weekly activation," Sylvie says, and closes her eyes.

Chloe sighs. "The therapist seems nice but she seems quite, you know, straight."

"I like straight," Sylvie says, sitting up, a smile breaking out.

Chloe laughs. "I think you fetishize straight. I do it too. It can be really attractive. But I think it would get boring pretty quick."

"I don't know. If it's a good feeling, would it be boring? Can feelings be boring?"

"Maybe not for babies," Chloe says.

"What?" Sylvie says, and starts laughing.

Chloe laughs and lies down in the pebbles, then sits up again, and her back is covered in dust. "You could just get a train into London, look at the men hanging around Frith Street Tattoo, to get your weekly activation. You used to do that, that used to work, right?"

Sylvie smiles. "It did," she says, sniffing.

"Or you could go to South Bank and watch all the skateboarders."

"Right," Sylvie says. "I could try that."

"It was never going to be forever," Chloe says. "You know that. People move, people leave, people even die. But *you* can be forever, for as long as you can think."

Sylvie nods, then rubs her wet nose on her knees.

"I can't believe she said, *It is what it is*, to you," Chloe says, sounding cross for once. "I would *never* say something like that to you."

"I know, I know you wouldn't," Sylvie whispers, smiling, and she leans to one side to pull out the goodbye card she's been sitting on.

"I mean, it *isn't* what it is," Chloe says. "It *isn't* what it is!" she says again, her tone sounding enraged.

Sylvie laughs, then she looks down and follows the loops of the therapist's handwriting on the envelope. When she sips more coffee, it goes down the wrong way, and she chokes, then starts to sob. She moves her body from side to side to dig herself down into the pebbles and covers her wet face with her arm. Chloe leans over Sylvie, and slowly and silently strokes her hair.

37

EVEN IN FICTION

SYLVIE WAKES AND STARES at the face on her Pierrot pillow-case. She turns the pillow over quickly so the side with a pattern of roses is uppermost, and wonders if she will let her-self think about the therapist as much as she wants today, since it's her first day post-therapy. Downstairs, she makes coffee, gets Curtains on a leash, and sets out for a walk before breakfast, hoping to see the therapist walking Butter.

On the hill, Sylvie allows herself to scan the back of the therapist's house as she walks. She thinks she can locate the narrow window of the therapy room, though she might be wrong, the back of the house is a complicated shape. Sylvie wonders what the therapist is doing in that room now that she isn't giving therapy sessions. She pictures her wearing gold, doing performance art on the chairs, and gasps and starts to laugh. Then she pictures the therapist's husband watching her, maybe with his friends, and straightaway stops laughing. When she puts Curtains's poo in the trash can, she lets the lid clang loudly and hopes the therapist's husband will hear. She wants him to know that she knows what might be going on upstairs in his house, although she knows that she doesn't.

Sylvie turns back home, Curtains trailing slowly behind her, and when they arrive at the front door, Sylvie thinks it has a dull, mocking look about it, like the door to the house of someone who overestimated their own importance, someone who thought her therapist would never want to stop their sessions. Sylvie carries Curtains over the threshold and when she puts her down, the dog picks her favorite Garfield toy up from the floor and carries it to her bed. The orange toy has grown hard and black with a silver sheen after years of being humped and licked by Curtains. It's disgusting how much she likes the toy, and it's disgusting what she's done to it, but it's sweet, Sylvie thinks, because Curtains is a dog.

Sylvie lies down on the sofa and calls Conrad.

"I'm no longer *in therapy*," Sylvie says.

"Congratulations," Conrad says. "Are you normal now?"

"Not really."

"It's good it's over. You seemed way too obsessed."

"It doesn't *feel* good. My life feels kind of empty."

"That's because you let your therapist be your whole world. You can't do that, you can't take someone else as the basis for your own life. You can only take yourself. Your therapist gets herself, and you get yourself. Everyone gets to base their own life on themselves."

"Right," Sylvie says.

"You wouldn't want someone else to base their life on you," Conrad says.

"No, I'd hate that. It seems obvious, the way you say it. I feel like if the therapist had said something like that, it might have snapped me out of it. It might have shifted something in my brain."

"Maybe she liked how obsessed you were?"

Sylvie snorts down the phone and smiles to herself and tries to control her smile.

"I just can't believe she doesn't care what I do now," Sylvie says. "I'm so used to reporting everything back to her, telling her how I've been. And if she doesn't care now, if she doesn't want to know how I've been . . . it seems unlikely she ever cared, or ever wanted to know."

"I think it's pretty unlikely that she ever cared. I don't think any therapists really care," Conrad says. "They're just . . . they're getting paid. I'm sure they're all just making a mental shopping list and pretending to listen the whole time."

Sylvie exhales slowly through a closed mouth, letting her lips puff out.

"So what are you going to do now?" Conrad says.

"I've been thinking about applying to therapy school," Sylvie says tentatively. Sylvie sits up and pictures the logo from the institute's website—the institute the therapist trained at. She imagines the logo on the pocket of her navy-blue blazer.

"Sylvie," Conrad says. "No," he says.

Sylvie feels like crying. "When I imagine myself training, I feel really in-the-world. It makes me feel so positive about the future."

"You're in the world already, at the vet's. And that seems to make sense for you. You like animals. When have you ever given a shit about other people?"

Sylvie grunts and her impulse to cry vanishes.

"Don't be cross with me," Conrad says.

"I'm not saying I'm doing it for other people," Sylvie says. "I'm doing it for me. So I feel like the kind of person that the therapist would want to talk to. I mean, so I feel like the therapist."

Conrad laughs.

"I did have another idea that might make me happy, that would take less time and be less expensive." Sylvie brings her feet up onto the sofa and hugs her knees with her free hand.

Conrad makes an encouraging noise.

"I could try to date a therapist. I could go on a dating site and specifically ask for a therapist."

"Can you do that? I mean, can they do that? Wouldn't they be struck off or something?"

"I'm not sure. Maybe I should just look for someone who'd be up for pretending to be a therapist, then."

"That sounds more sensible," Conrad says.

"Would you do something like that?" Sylvie remembers a photo of her and Conrad when they were flatmates. Just about to go out, Conrad wearing a cardigan, Sylvie carrying a small sparkling handbag, their underwear hung up to dry on the radiator behind them.

"Like what?"

"Meet up with me in a small, square room—we could hire one—and sit in a chair opposite me. And then listen, or pretend to listen, and cross your legs, nod, repeat things I say every now and then."

Conrad laughs. "What would I have to wear?"

"You could wear whatever you want. But probably you'd wear a brown cardigan, a white shirt, brown trousers, leather brogues—Church's or Tricker's."

Conrad snorts.

"I'd tell you a few key phrases to say. Like: *I can't hug you but I can 'hold' you.*"

"Jesus," Conrad says.

"Then—this is where it gets good—you could encourage me to sit on your lap or similar, and we could start to make out. You'd have to have things ready to say like, *It's normal to idealize your therapist*, if you sensed I was flagging."

"You remember that I'm married," Conrad says.

"Right," Sylvie says. She gets up and walks toward the bay window and looks out at the street. "Sorry. I wasn't meaning actually, really. I was just meaning in theory."

"You'll find someone to do it with. You can do what you want nowadays, you just type whatever it is into the internet."

Sylvie imagines large men in crumpled checked shirts hovering over their laptops, replying to her with thick, hairy fingers, smiling, breathing heavily. "I don't know if I could do that in reality. Though I did type the dog idea into the internet already."

"The dog idea," Conrad says.

"I told you about it. My idea of going into the body of the therapist's dog so I could do all the things I want to do."

"Right," Conrad says.

"It's obviously impossible," Sylvie says.

"Some people would think it so impossible they wouldn't get to the stage of saying: *It's obviously impossible.*"

Sylvie snorts. "Do you remember when you lent me *The Island of Dr. Moreau?*"

"Did I? I don't remember. I love that book."

"It was too dark for me," Sylvie says. "I can handle that kind of stuff at work, opening animals up, seeing their insides, but only when it's to save the animal."

"I mean, it's fiction," Conrad says. "I wouldn't want to see animal experiments in real life."

"No, I know," Sylvie says. "But even in fiction, I struggled."

"Anyway, don't you cut dogs' balls off at work? That's not saving them."

"But it saves them to not have urges they can't act on. If you're sitting on someone's sofa watching a crappy TV show . . . it must make it slightly less frustrating if these urges you can't act on have been taken away."

Conrad laughs. "Maybe," he says. "I still don't think I'd like it. Look, why don't you come over soon? We used to see you all the time before you got together with Owen. Come and have dinner. I have a VR headset now."

38

FORTUNE COOKIE

SYLVIE PUTS ON HER BISCUIT-COLORED CARDIGAN. She'd bought the cardigan when the therapist had gone on holiday for three weeks. She'd zoomed in on the therapist's cardigan in her LinkedIn profile and searched for a similar shade online. She'd hoped that when she put it on, she'd feel the slow calmness of the aftermath of the therapist's beauty. She pulls at the sleeves. Somehow her cardigan has never been enough like the therapist's cardigan. Sylvie's cardigan feels like a child's cardigan somehow, though it isn't, she had gotten it from the women's section, not the children's.

I should have asked for the therapist's LinkedIn cardigan, as a goodbye present, she texts Chloe.

Chloe texts back with a teary-face emoji.

At the time, I felt like asking her for an egg.

You wanted to grow her baby? Chloe replies.

I meant those eggs made of precious stone, Sylvie says. *Should have said.*

Chloe sends a broken heart emoji.

I think I'm going to try the takeaway-in-a-sleeping-bag thing tonight, Sylvie says. *I want to do a ritual, and put something in myself. I feel like an empty vessel.*

You're not an empty vessel.

Sometimes it feels like I've lost everything, now I've lost the therapist.

Sylvie, I feel worried about you. Listen to me: you've lost nothing, and you don't need to change. You've already reached perfection.

Sylvie shakes her head.

I'm going up to my mum's for a few days tomorrow, Chloe says. *For her birthday. But let's meet when I get back?*

OK, Sylvie replies.

Let's meet again and again, Chloe says, *over and over and over and over, and never stop.*

OK! Sylvie replies, adding a smiling-face emoji.

Sylvie ties Curtains up outside the Chinese restaurant and goes inside to collect her order. A TV is playing some kind of soap opera in warm colors, and alternating cans of Coke and Pepsi are lined up underneath a Chinese zodiac calendar. Sylvie leans in to check the calendar while she waits—it's the Year of the Dog. She adds a Pepsi and a Coke to her order, she wants to see how different she feels with each one.

She's already put the backseats of her car down. She's

taken the car to the car wash and it's clean inside and there's a new air freshener hanging from the mirror that smells of bubble gum. She has the audio of the art exorcism downloaded on her phone, and she's packed her Pierrot sleeping bag. The Pierrots on the sleeping bag look like children, their suits are red and white and they're picking flowers. Sylvie drives to town with Curtains. She wants this trip to feel monumental. It feels stupid so far, but she suspects that could just be a stage something monumental has to go through. She parks under a streetlight and takes the key out of the ignition, activates the central locking with her elbow, and climbs into the back. She has a spoon in her pocket and she lays out the trays and starts eating. She opens a can of Coke. Curtains is curled up, watching.

Sylvie wonders if she should have parked outside the therapist's house, between the therapist's black shining car and the therapist's husband's fast car. But she needs to be relaxed when she does this thing she's about to do. She presses play. For a moment she wishes this was the first time she'd heard the song, she wishes she hadn't heard it when she still had the therapist as her therapist. But then she imagines doing this regularly, every week, a new kind of appointment. She turns the volume down, lifts Curtains onto her lap, gets the index card out of her pocket, and starts to read out the spell.

In the name of Panhu and Wiro ku, and Goofy the anthropomorphic dog.

In the name of Cerberus, Anubis, and Fenrir . . . I invoke all these names.

I call upon their powers to start a transformation, to cast out the appendix!

Out, non-functioning Jacobson's organ, out!
Out, cone-dominated retina, out!
Out, inability to see UV light, out!
Out, disappearing of the tail at eight weeks, out!
Out, verbal communication . . . you're no great loss.
Supernumerary phantom limb, don't cling to me, golden worm
in the ear, come into my mind . . . this is a bad species, after all.

When the audio ends, Sylvie opens a Pepsi and wonders if she's having fun. She puts the rice she hasn't eaten in front of Curtains and opens a tray of butter chicken for her. She watches Curtains eat while she sips her Pepsi. The Pepsi makes her feel like she's in a different country, or that she's more male, than the Coke does. She catches her reflection in the car window; it seems really far away. It looks nice, but it doesn't look like what's inside her. Sylvie wonders what Chloe sees when she looks at her, why she keeps meeting up with her. If Chloe sees something good when she looks at her, is she seeing Sylvie's past, or her future? She doesn't think she can be seeing her in the present, because in the present, her form is too amorphous.

Sylvie leaves Curtains eating in the back and climbs into the driver's seat to head home. When she drives past the therapist's house, she sees a free parking space opposite. She can hear her heart beat in her head suddenly, but she does it, she slows to a stop, parallel with the therapist's husband's car, and then reverse-parks into the space. She turns the engine off, but leaves the key in the ignition. She tries to keep her face calm and neutral, lets go of the steering wheel, and climbs into the back of the car. Curtains is snuffling in the trays, her face covered in rice. Sylvie gets into the sleeping bag and when she's lying inside it, with just her face exposed, she looks out of the window. There are lights on in the therapist's house. She makes fists with both hands and feels a fortune cookie in her right hand. She tears it open, breaks the cookie in half, gives one half to Curtains. She takes a foil-wrapped package from her pocket—it's the cookies the therapist gave her, broken into pieces. They're soft now, but she puts a section in her mouth to join the half of the fortune cookie, then opens up the fortune. It says:

YOU MUST TRY, OR HATE YOURSELF FOR NOT TRYING

39

FLOATING MINDS

AND SHE *HAD* TRIED: Sylvie feels certain she can categorize the writing of the spell, and the saying it out loud, and the mixing of the cookies, as trying. But after she'd swallowed, she'd heard the sound of a front door opening, and looked over to see the therapist's husband jogging down the path toward her car, Butter off-leash at his heels. Sylvie had ducked down, blood had drained from her face in fear, then she'd clumsily climbed back into the front, to drive the short distance home as soon as the coast was clear.

Sylvie wakes the next morning with a dry mouth, and goes to get a glass of water, though she never usually drinks water, not when she's by herself, she never feels that she needs it. She steps in a puddle made by Curtains as she crosses the kitchen, but she doesn't care, doesn't dry her feet, just tracks wet footprints all the way to her front door. It's sunny, and Sylvie sits down on the step outside her house with her glass of water, settles Curtains by her side.

She lifts her face up to the sun and closes her eyes. She didn't actually think the spell would work, not really. She didn't even have the right dog in the car with her! It was Butter she needed to swap with, not Curtains. Plus, Curtains had already been taken by her dad, she's pretty sure of that. A real scientist would have got the right equipment ready. Sylvie had acted like the whole thing was an art performance, not a science experiment.

Her phone buzzes and it's Chloe. She's sent Sylvie an audio file from the show she'd curated, the show Sylvie had enjoyed so much. The title of the file is "Medusa's Song."

I'm sending this to help you get over the therapist, Chloe texts her.

Sylvie plays the song. It sounds like the performer with long hair singing, her voice is as low as longing could make it. The song sounds too good to Sylvie, especially combined with the feeling of sunlight, so she presses pause during the first verse and goes inside to make coffee. She wants to prepare herself for something this good, and then she wants to make it even better, by herself.

Sitting outside again, with coffee and water, Sylvie presses play. *"Pale and Young, I'm at your service . . ."*

She texts Chloe: *"I'm at your service!"* I did always want to be the therapist's PA, follow her round, bring her coffee. I always used to tell her that.

And what did she say? Chloe replies.

She told me I should bring MYSELF coffee.

Sylvie looks over at the empty road and her heart sinks. She wants the therapist to drive past now, in her special black car. She feels she needs just a quick glimpse of her. A dark car pulls up then across the road, but it isn't the therapist's car, it's the myHermes delivery car, and really more dark blue than black. A lady wearing jeans gets out and crosses the road, hands a gray package to Sylvie. Sylvie tears it open straight-away: it's the out-of-print book about countertransference that she'd ordered: *The Intimate Hour*. Sylvie looks at the black-and-white photograph of a therapist's couch on the cover, reads the subtitle, *Love and Sex in Psychotherapy*, laughs quickly, then sits back against the doorjamb and plays the song Chloe sent her again, from the beginning. The piano is sad and slow and Sylvie pictures the therapist sitting in the back row at a crematorium, on a velvet padded chair that's dull, burgundy, and sagging. She texts Chloe again:

Maybe I'll use this Medusa song for my funeral.

Chloe replies with a bandaged heart emoji and a candle emoji.

Instead of "All Cats Are Grey," Sylvie adds.

Sylvie wants to text more, discuss the pros and cons of each song, but she feels too stuck inside her sadness to talk, like a baby in the womb not yet ready to come out. Curtains has been inching her way toward the book, and is now chewing one corner, turning it into gray pulp. Sylvie watches. She knows she has good things around her: Curtains, coffee, sunshine, texts from Chloe, a new book to read, but it's not enough: she still feels she'd rather die if she can't see the therapist again. She stretches out her arms, then twists them to look at their soft white undersides. There are no scars—she supposes she never cut deep enough—but she used to buy razor blades and plasters with her sushi on lunch hour when things started to go wrong with Sandy. She'd slide the edge of a blade along her arm when she got home, sitting on the bathroom floor, while she made herself think hard about the fact that Sandy had stopped loving her. Then she'd apply a plaster, like a mother, and feel better. The equipment was all so small it could fit in a pencil case, and all her movements seemed neat and right. It felt good to transform the pain in her heart into something she could see: little balls of blood, coming up all in a row. She starts to trace the therapist's name along her arm, gently, with the back of a fingernail. Could she still do it now?

I want the therapist to have to come to my funeral, she texts Chloe quickly. *Soon, and for the rest of her life.*

The message doesn't go through, the one tick doesn't change to two. *Nobody cares that I'm in hell*, Sylvie thinks, watching Curtains chewing the book. Sylvie looks up at the road again and, for a few minutes, considers shaving her head.

40

CAROUSEL

SYLVIE GETS INTO BED, though it's just the afternoon, and stares at the Canis Major picture on her wall. She wants to sleep, so she can stop feeling, but she can't because something like hot poison seems to be flowing inside her arms. She feels like her body doesn't want to be a body for her, and her bed doesn't want her to lie in it. She rolls over, finds her phone, and plays "Medusa's Song." *Try to enjoy not enjoying yourself,* Sylvie thinks. She wonders, for what seems like the millionth time, why humans were made with brains that don't serve them well, why consciousness feels like a trap. She remembers her boss at the bookshop talking about his favorite ending in a novel. It was the ending of *Venus on the Half-Shell,* when the wise man Bingo is asked why life was created, just so that billions would suffer for no reason, and his answer is: "Why not?"

Sylvie gets out of bed. Her feet are still sticky from Curtains's puddle, and she runs herself a shallow bath, quietly chants, "Why not? Why not? Why not?" as she scrubs her soles. When she drives to town, her arms still feel pumped up with poison, her body is heavy to move. She goes straight to Argos, flicks to the jewelry section in the giant catalogue, finds a gold ankle chain, and hands in her order. When her box comes down the chute, she rips it open and puts the chain straight on, over her white ribbed sock.

On her way to look for leg warmers, Sylvie unlocks her phone, tells Chloe that she's shopping for a different uniform, in the indoor shopping center.

I never thought that I would find myself in bed amongst the stones, Chloe replies, quoting "All Cats Are Grey" in response to Sylvie's last message, and commenting, Sylvie is sure, on how it feels to be inside the shopping center. Sylvie's body starts to lighten.

She types: *Do you know what the phrase "all cats are grey in the dark" actually means?*

Chloe replies that she doesn't.

It's been my favourite song for years, but I never knew what it meant, and I looked it up the other day. It means, I think, that it doesn't matter who you have sex with, when you do it in the dark. It doesn't matter what they look like, it doesn't matter who it is.

Sylvie is at the heavy glass doors of the shopping complex, and uses both hands to open them. Couples and big families—

people she doesn't usually see—are walking around, all wearing different colors and shapes of clothing. It looks messy and confusing, and Sylvie's eyes move past them and land on a figure leaning against the gumball machines. Dressed in black and brown, they remind Sylvie of a German shepherd. A teenager, she supposes, but she can't tell what gender. There are gray hospital-issue crutches propped up on the machine next to them, but they aren't using them—their hands are full, a phone in one, a book in the other. When Sylvie gets nearer she sees that the book is *Demian* by Hermann Hesse. Something shifts in Sylvie's brain.

I've just seen the teenage me, she texts Chloe. *The same clothes, the same book.*

I'll try to get a photo, she adds.

When she opens the camera up on her phone, the teenager looks up, scowls at her. They have brown hair, in curtains, and when they bring up their hand to smooth it, Sylvie sees a flash of the strap of a neon yellow watch. She switches from the camera back to messaging.

Jesus, she texts Chloe. *They even have the same watch I had. This neon yellow watch, that always cheered me up.*

My watch used to cheer me up too! Chloe replies straightaway. *Why is that? Time passing, things changing?*

Sylvie lets out a laugh. She's in the middle of the shopping center, standing in place, and she stretches her arms up above her, then brings her hands down onto her head, pushing her hair over her face for a minute. She looks across at the teenager, they are sitting cross-legged on the floor now, reading the book.

Sylvie walks toward the figure, then stops halfway and

stands behind a carousel of gift pens. The pens have a selection of boys' and girls' names printed on them in blue and pink script, and are arranged in alphabetical order. Sylvie turns the carousel slowly, scanning the names on the pens with one eye, watching the figure reading *Demian* with the other. First she looks for the therapist's name on the pens, and it's there, but seeing it doesn't make her shake, or even feel particularly lucky. Next she looks for a "Chloe" pen, quickly finds one, and considers buying it, but thinks Chloe will already have one. She looks for her own name then, and there's a space for it, but there are no pens there, it's out of stock. Sylvie keeps spinning the carousel. *My situation goes round and round*, she thinks, still watching the teenager. Sylvie wants to know why they are sitting in the shopping center to read, and surprises herself by thinking she might be able to work it out, if she waits and watches them awhile. They lift the paperback higher then so it completely obscures their face, and Sylvie looks at the frayed cuffs of their brown cardigan, which seem chewed. Sylvie remembers chewing her cardigan cuffs when she was nervous at school, the wool getting heavy with spit. Then she remembers her dad calling her Charlie at the dinner table when she wore it, after Charlie Chaplin's character the Little Tramp.

41

A MILLION YEARS

THE FOLLOWING WEEK, the therapist's LinkedIn profile disappears from the internet. Sylvie calls Chloe: "The therapist isn't a therapist anymore," she says.

On a Saturday evening, Sylvie picks up Chloe, then drives her back to Sylvie's, and they stop to collect Chinese food on the way. When Sylvie drives past the therapist's house, she slows down and glances over at Chloe, to see if she's trying to see inside.

"I never see the lights on anymore," Sylvie says. "It's like she never even existed."

"But *we* know she existed," Chloe says.

"The therapist was here," Sylvie says flatly, driving round the corner.

———

Sylvie lays the food out on the table in the lounge: egg fried rice, chips, butter chicken, salt-and-pepper tofu, two cans of Coke. Chloe is standing in front of a tall bookshelf, her head at an angle scanning the titles, Curtains walking slowly in circles around the room.

"How come we've never done this before?" Sylvie says, smiling, as she pours Coke into two glasses.

"I'm too busy, I guess," Chloe says, pulling out a book to look at the cover. "I'm always working in the evenings."

Sylvie nods and makes a soft noise of assent.

When Chloe's eyes reach the bottom of the bookshelf, she pulls out a purple ring binder that has a picture on the spine of Pierrot holding a rose.

"I had this exact same folder!" she says, turning to Sylvie.

"That's my therapy folder!" Sylvie says, blushing a little. She takes it from Chloe, puts it on her lap, flicks through it as they begin to eat.

"I'll read out the good bits for you," she says.

Chloe smiles, starts on her chicken.

"God," Sylvie says as she flicks through. "I can't find a single thing worth reading out."

Chloe laughs. "The only interesting part was the fantasy," she says.

"Here's a good bit, about Nick," Sylvie says then. "It's about the time I told him I was depressed, and he said I should write him a letter about it. I spent all day writing the letter, it was teenage, very intense, all about how hard it was to be me,

I suppose. Being forced to eat chicken, being scoffed at for crying. And when I went round to his house that evening and tried to give it to him, he told me to put it back in my pocket."

"He didn't even read it?" Chloe says.

"No!" Sylvie says, laughing and shaking her head.

"My god," Chloe says. "And what did the therapist say about that?"

"I don't think I told her about it in the end," Sylvie says. She sips some Coke, then says, "I was so impressed with Nick that time. I thought: *Nobody's going to be able to top that.* And nobody has, I don't think."

Chloe drinks more Coke, then asks if Sylvie has a photo of Nick, asks if she can see it, and Sylvie leads Chloe to the bottom of the stairs where Nick's funeral card is hung in a small white frame.

After a few seconds standing in silence, staring at the card, they return to the lounge to finish their meal. Sylvie picks up Curtains, puts her on the sofa between them, and the dog circles, then lies down facing away from the TV. Sylvie sets up the film that Chloe has brought for them to watch: *Picnic at Hanging Rock.* They both have a wrapped fortune cookie in their hand, and they read the closed captions as they watch the opening credits: *What we see, and what we seem, are but a dream . . . a dream within a dream.* There are girls in white lace, waking up, opening windows, reading out poems to each other, then washing their faces in basins filled with flowers.

"I think this is how my friend Charlotte imagined me living, when we were sixteen," Sylvie says, and Chloe laughs.

When Miranda, brushing her hair in the mirror, tells her friend that she must learn to love someone else, since she won't be here much longer, Sylvie makes a pained expression, and grips Chloe's arm.

"I nearly changed my name to Miranda, because of her," Chloe whispers.

They keep watching. A teacher in a small black hat talks about the lava being forced up from deep down below, a million years ago, and the schoolgirl Irma jokes, *Waiting a million years, just for us.* A teacher in white suddenly realizes that Miranda is a Botticelli angel. Then, when Miranda, trance-like, says, *Everything begins and ends at exactly the right time and place*, Sylvie gasps and looks over at Chloe, who seems to be holding her breath.

"You do know how much Nick looks like the therapist," Chloe says then, as if it has just occurred to her. Sylvie turns her gaze back to the TV. She digs her hand under Curtains to try to find the remote, but when she gets it out from under her and presses pause, the film doesn't stop.

"The button's worn out," Sylvie whispers, "or the battery's dead."

She keeps pressing the button for a while longer, trying to pause the film, but it keeps playing, so she stops trying, and submits to the film. When the girls exploring the rock quietly lie down together, Chloe and Sylvie too shuffle down, at opposite ends of the sofa, bending their knees to accommodate Curtains.

"This has been my favorite film since I was seventeen," Chloe says. "I knew you'd like it too."

Sylvie cracks her cookie open with her teeth, and reads out the fortune: *"Lead by example, not by words alone."* Chloe rolls her eyes and goes next. *"Love is right around the corner,"* she reads out, her tone incredulous.

42

CHERUB CLOTHING

SYLVIE IS SITTING at the kitchen table with a third cup of coffee. It is day thirteen of not having the therapist as her therapist. Yesterday, on day twelve, Sylvie had been successful in not texting her. She had started three messages after Chloe had left, but had been able to press the back arrow. It had seemed justifiable to text, because Sylvie had still not worked out what the therapist had said when they'd hugged, and maybe it had been important. But even when the sky had started to get dark, and the text had started to feel urgent, Sylvie hadn't sent it. She had caught sight of her reflection in a framed picture at the top of the stairs, and her eyes had seemed to be saying: *Show her that you love her by* not *texting her, that's the best way to show your love.*

Sylvie takes a sip of coffee and keeps scrolling through the clothing website she has up on her phone. She looks at the items of clothing made in different shapes to fit different parts of the human body but all with the same picture: two cherubs, one with blond hair, one with brown. The cherubs are resting their chins on their arms, they look bored on their clouds, they look like they have been waiting a long time for someone, like they're still waiting. Sylvie clicks on a baseball hat, thinking she could do with extra protection from the sun, though it's not something she'd normally wear. But how did she get onto this site with the cherub clothing? *Is this how things are manifested nowadays?* Sylvie thinks, not knowing exactly what she means.

Sylvie carries Curtains outside. She lowers her to the pavement and they walk slowly together toward the hill. The street is very quiet.

"Curtains," Sylvie says, looking down. "We have food, shelter, and what is the third thing that everybody needs?"

Sylvie takes her phone out of her pocket to search for support groups for people quitting therapy, but the only thing that comes up is available therapists. It feels like the only time Sylvie has googled something and not found it, found its opposite instead. Sylvie lets Curtains off the leash in the middle of the green and scans all around for the therapist, but doesn't see her. Although Sylvie can see the therapist's house from the corner of her eye, she tries not to look at it directly. "What we see or what we seem . . ." Sylvie begins, then she stops, wondering if the therapist would be able to see her from her house, if she would be able to lip-read from that distance. But the therapist wouldn't be looking out for her, and anyway, she couldn't care less if she saw Sylvie talking to herself, now that she's not a paying client. A small white dog darts past, cutting in front of Curtains, and Sylvie checks its dimensions but the legs are too short, the fur is too curly, the ears are too long, it isn't Butter.

When a pink cloud moves over the sun, Sylvie picks up Curtains, puts her down again facing home, and they start to walk back together. Sylvie gets out her phone then and starts a text, typing quickly, almost frantically, while walking slowly at the pace of a funeral procession.

I can't believe I can never speak to you again, she types.

Sylvie spins in a circle and checks the green again. She looks at all the human figures standing around talking to each other and at all the dogs running, making happy shapes, then she puts Curtains back on the leash and sends the text. *The text has gone to her*, Sylvie thinks, *it's gone to the therapist, into her phone, because our phones are in the same world, because there is only one world.*

THANK YOU

My lovely daughter, Fawn, for being so caring, and for promising not to read this book.

Seren Adams, guardian angel agent, for caring and advocating so much *out of nowhere*.

Catherine Wood for understanding, for your brilliant brain, for friendship, and for showing me Anne Imhof and Mark Leckey.

Sheila Heti for existing and for being so kind to me.

Mitzi Angel for the insight and magic guidance.

Na Kim for the beautiful Pierrot painting.

Kishani Widyaratna for such support and fun chats.

Chelsea Hodson, dream writing teacher, for "Finish What You Start" and filling my Saturday nights with fun workshops.

Makenna Goodman for the brilliant "Cultivating Obsession" workshop.

Hannah Vincent for the heartening classes in Brighton.

Elle Nash for being so generous, with advice and friendship.

Likewise Marta Balcewicz, for giving much needed advice and support.

Elizabeth Ellen for lovely encouraging emails.

Daisuke Shen for the fun class with Mr. Bean and then the encouraging Zoom.

Madeline Cash and Anika Jade Levy for publishing my first story online at *Forever Magazine*.

Sarah Taylor Jackson and Emma Leard Jackson for being such encouraging first readers.

Arielle McManus for encouraging me to start sending out my writing.

Jordan Teear for talking about Henry Miller, Cormac McCarthy, and Hermann Hesse at my tattoo appointments, unknowingly being the antidote I needed to bad things happening then. I love my permanent teardrop.

Mark Leckey for the inspiration I got from his brilliant *Exorcism of the Bridge@Eastham Rake*.

Anne Imhof for the crazy-enjoyable show *Sex* at the Tate Modern.

Alessandro Raho for his magic paintings.

Charlie Crabb and Elliot Martin at the Hastings Bookshop. So nice that Elliot agreed to do my readings while I stood nearby, just like my sister in church.

Guy Bolongaro for talking about the Cure, *Journey to the End of the Night*, and *Drive* while taking photos.

Sam Herlihy of Hope Of The States for the use of lyrics, and for the years of joy your beautiful songs have brought me.

Lucy Lee, Nick Kilroy, Mathew Sawyer, Jon Butterworth, Sarah Pickles, Alice Martin, Howard Mollett, Dino Gollnick, Amber Cowan, Isabella Fiore-Brown, Graeme Wilson, and my writing class friends.

Thank you, Mum, full of love, thank you, therapist, full of kindness.

A Note About the Author

Adelaide Faith worked as an editor at Channel 4 Learning before training to be a veterinary nurse at Battersea Dogs and Cats Home, after which she worked as a nurse at the Royal Society for the Prevention of Cruelty to Animals and the People's Dispensary for Sick Animals. Her short fiction has appeared in *Forever Magazine, Hobart, Vol. 1 Brooklyn, Maudlin House, Farewell Transmission, ExPat Press*, and *Vlad Mag*. She is a member of Chelsea Hodson's Morning Writing Club, and she lives in Hastings, England, with her daughter and dogs.